Emma H.

by the Author

as Keith Botsford
The Mothers
Out of Nowhere
The Master Race
The Eighth-Best-Dressed Man in the World
Benvenuto
The March-Man
Editors (with Saul Bellow)

as I.I. Magdalen
The Search for Anderson
Lennie & Vance & Benji

I.I. Magdalen

Emma H.

The Toby Press

The Toby Press
First Edition 2003

The Toby Press LLC
www.tobypress.com

Copyright © I.I. Magdalen, 2003

The right of Keith Botsford to be identified as the author of this work has been asserted by him in accordance with the Copyright, Designs & Patents Act 1988

All rights reserved. No part of this publication may be reproduced, stored in a retrieval system or transmitted in any form or by any means, electronic, mechanical, photocopying or otherwise, without the prior permission of the publisher, except in the case of brief quotations embodied in critical articles or reviews.

This is a work of fiction. The characters, incidents, and dialogues are products of the author's imagination and are not to be construed as real. Any resemblance to actual events or persons, living or dead is entirely coincidental.

ISBN 1 902881 67 2 paperback original

A CIP catalogue record for this title is available from the British Library

Typeset in Garamond by Jerusalem Typesetting

Printed and bound in the United States by Thomson-Shore Inc., Michigan

The Toby Crime Series
Introduction

As Georges Simenon once remarked, all of us, brought to extremity by a sudden change in circumstance, can be compelled into a situation in which crime seems the only possible way out. Crime novels, then, are about such extremes of human behavior and they exist in all literatures. The French call them *noirs*; in Italy they are *gialli*; we used to call them "detective stories" or "mysteries", and most English and American ones have centered on the "puzzle" or "low life" aspect. But what has brought many remarkable novelists (Dostoyevsky, Balzac, Wilkie Collins, Graham Greene) to the genre is, I suspect, not so much the solution of a puzzle, but the fact that extremities clarify human dilemmas and afford the writer a clear narrative to follow. For a century-and-a-half, readers everywhere have enjoyed them for those same reasons.

Whatever the type, all crime (or "espionage") novels, from Buchan through Le Carré, rest (to different degrees), on action and character, and involve suspense. Suspense derives from not knowing how something will work out—hence the "thriller" which compels readers to turn the pages. But there is a substantial difference—it is a

Emma H.

matter of the emphasis placed on character and language—between the least of these (many of which afford pleasure) and those which engage the reader at a higher level, whose pleasures are richer and more lasting.

Toby Crime proposes a series in which crime novels from many literatures are first novels, and only then crime novels. That is, they are written for a literate public by writers who engage with language and society, and pose genuine human dilemmas. In that sense they go beyond crime to real life and real characters. The crime will not always be murder and they will come in all shapes and sizes, though the majority will be short. I like to think they would have been enjoyed by Simenon, Greene and Chandler, as by Ian Rankin, Henning Mankell and Elmore Leonard, among other contemporary masters of the genre.

KEITH BOTSFORD,
General Editor

Author's Preface

The events described in Emma H. took place in Belgium during and immediately after the Second World War.

The Belgium created in 1830 out of territory that had in the past been Frankish, Burgundian, Hapsburg, French and Dutch has long been socially and culturally divided between French and Catholic (Walloon) Belgium and Flemish and Protestant Belgium, with an additional German component added after the 1914–1918 war. Thus, in different areas of Belgium the predominant language spoken has differed. Liège (or Luik), in which much of Emma H. takes place, was once a Bishopric and is Belgium's second city.

In the period before the Second World War, Belgium—like its French neighbor—suffered from unstable parliamentary governments. The Rexist party (after 'Rex', for 'Christ the King'), led by Léon Degrelle, started life in 1935 as an anti-parliamentary, anti-communist 'national front'. A similar Flemish group, the Flemish National League, had been formed in 1933. By 1936, the Rexists—populist and vaguely socialist—held 21 seats in the Belgian parliament. Its decline began in 1938 when the principal traditional parties united to defeat it.

Emma H.

The Germans invaded Belgium in 1940; King Leopold was deported to Germany after the Belgian capitulation. Resistance to the Germans and Nazis was difficult and dangerous in a small country, and the resistance itself was divided into its linguistic, cultural and religious parts, with political differences causing further fragmentation. Some collaboration with the Germans was inevitable because of Nazi control of the Belgian economy. Collaboration with the enemy was no greater (and no lesser) than French collaboration, but many in Flemish Belgium felt a racial affinity with the German conqueror.

When the country was liberated in 1944, a few of its major collaborators were executed; others were imprisoned. Degrelle himself had joined the Flemish Legion that fought alongside the Nazis in Russia. At the end of the war, he flew his own plane to San Sebastian in Spain where he found safe haven under the Franco regime.

1983

Chapter one

Emma H—? Well, Henning Forsell said—as if it were a matter of no great importance—she was all of nineteen when she was killed. Murdered, the old lady says, executed is what I hear around. Real name, Emma Hoofrad. Listed as Emma H. out of regard for social susceptibilities. Rich family, prominent people, but not really from here.

He didn't say how the old lady, Emma's aunt, had importuned him: written him, called him, telegraphed him, sent her lawyer after him. How she wasn't to be put off.

Either way, he continued, very dead for some time, since 1945 is thirty-eight years ago and you and I didn't even exist.

She thought, queer man I've married. To her, thirty-three might have seemed old—if she hadn't fallen in love so abruptly. And with a man who didn't usually talk that much.

Henning said, The old lady won't see me. Not in person. She does everything through her *notaire* in Liège, Luik, whatever you want to call the place. A certain Jacques Coquin. You know what those people—*notaires*, not old ladies—are like. Cheat you blind with respectability. At least the French ones do. The man's name means something like a cute rogue. A rogue he probably is. Cute, no.

'Enning (she couldn't pronounce that opening 'h', hotels were 'otels), stop. You are trying to tell me something. At the same time you wish to distract me, is that right?

Yes, I'm telling you about this girl who was killed. The girl was her beloved niece, she was killed, *Mevrouw* Kerkevelde isn't satisfied, and because Emma's case has, let's say, 'political' overtones—something an Italian like you would understand—no Belgian will take up her cause. Apparently I'm it. Why, I wouldn't know.

I see. You told me already, sometimes you will leave me for a while.

Not for long.

Henning was talking to his new wife Ludi (for Ludovica) in the very sort of place she hated most, a place where it rained all the time, even in summer, where you couldn't get a decent espresso, the tiled roofs drove you crazy with their patterns, the red brick of the houses dripped with the constant drizzle and unseen eyes were—you knew—peering out at you from behind lace curtains.

He'd had to pretend a bit, of course, to get her to Belgium at all, by suggesting the Formula One race at Spa/Francorchamps and then this little corner of Limburg. Because in *Mevrouw* Kerkevelde's first letter—it had reached him in London several weeks before his miraculous meeting with Ludi—she had sent him a photograph of the girl and that had been that. He had known right away he wouldn't refuse.

So he suggested the track because Ludi knew one of the drivers. More especially his wife Rita with whom Ludi had done her *Liceo*.

So the two girls and Henning had sat around freezing under umbrellas at the plastic tables outside the motor home and the girls had enjoyed a good gossip. Then, some time after Henning, (cars were not his thing, made too much noise), Ludi had got bored—she regularly got bored, twenty-one-year-olds often do—and they'd fled the track and the rain by a back road, even before practice started.

I.I. Magdalen

Of course Henning chaffed her. He said, If you hadn't wanted to go swanning around the grand prix we wouldn't be in such a dump.

You said, we will go to Spa. We are here because of this girl.

A little.

Ludi smiled. She said, Already I know you like to sniff around. Next time not in Belgium please.

Rio, I promise.

Then she put her head back and fell asleep.

She was not wrong. Somewhere hereabouts was the crime scene. He'd been given directions. A garage, a country road (paved) and then a right turn into a much narrower road (gravel) which led up to a cabin. If he came to a quarry he'd gone too far.

Though what you might find there after all these years stumps me, his Brussels banking friend had said.

At least the trail won't have been trampled all over.

No one gives a damn.

The girl's aunt does.

You should ask why.

Vindication?

He found the garage. A sort of general store with two pumps outside.

They went in and bought execrable coffee in paper cups under a Picasso peace poster and another picturing America and a swastika. Not the sort of thing you find in most garages.

The owner—sixtyish and burly—was disobliging. The look he gave them before putting on his pea jacket and going out to do his job on the car said that he never willingly sold fuel or bad coffee at all to Walloons, or any French speakers for that matter.

Henning didn't ask about the quarry or Emma. It's a complicated country, he told Ludi.

Populated by boors, Ludi answered. Let's get out.

They'd been married three months and when they got back in the car, unexpectedly Henning went on talking. She liked it when he talked.

She found it urbane and often funny. *Inglesi* and *americani* had a very different sense of humor from Italians. She also thought her husband was nervous with women. Talk calmed him down, as did having something to do.

He talked, but he didn't say why he'd been fascinated, sucked in, by the photograph of Emma the old woman had shown him. Though it was obvious to her he had been.

Emma would be fifty-five now, Henning said. I'd think she'd look pretty much as she did then. A beauty, a real beauty. Generations of Flemish, Dutch blood making for sandy blonde hair that must once have been like flax. And the most extraordinary high forehead, like the ones you always go on about in Flemish paintings.

Like the landscape, it was discreet, that forehead. He'd been places where the landscape sought to impose—a matter of mass, or bulk, or obviousness—and really liked the domestic character of Flanders in general. It suited.

So much forehead, Ludi replied. It can be very lovely.

Indeed. But very severe. Wouldn't suit you.

I'm hungry.

I promise you we'll eat in Liège or Luik, whichever you like. You choose. Tremendous food in either place.

Silly man, she said with affection. Still, she really didn't want to be stuck in Belgium one day longer than she had to. She added, I know you're going to come back here tomorrow and leave me abandoned in the hotel.

In her view, the country wasn't merely complicated, with its rotten history and its two languages—French, which Belgians spoke badly and Flemish, the other, incomprehensible, like old men clearing their throats, it was also deeply uncivilized. No sunshine, no decent coffee. Plus the awful hats the women wore, the mountains of food they consumed, that spurious domesticity, the dark, beer-smelling bars, the ill-lit streets. How did anyone manage to live in a village such as they'd stopped in, without shops or sunlight, basically squatting on top of seams of coal?

I.1. Magdalen

He took her hand. He said, I'll give you the facts up front. You be the judge and you tell me if I should be interested.

Why else would we be here if you weren't interested?

Implacable feminine logic and a clever girl. Henning often felt that women made him transparent. They seemed to be able to read his mind.

He said, here's what I know about Emma, besides the fact that she was a great beauty. The general view is that she was a *volunteer*. As far back as 1942, when she was sixteen and a model student. That is, she signed on with the other side, with the enemy.

Her aunt told you that?

No. Her aunt said I would soon enough find out the *pretext* that was used to murder her. She said her niece was not perfect.

It was a love affair? said Ludi.

That would be nice, but not even in Protestant countries do they execute you for love. Besides, she sounds as if she was a bit aloof, certainly serious. But she didn't take up with the Germans for any advantage she could get out of it, she didn't profiteer, go round in nylons and furs. She was an accomplished pianist, she read a lot, she came from a comfortable family. So why did she join the wrong side? If she did.

The wrong side is the losing side, Ludi said. My mother's older brother only just escaped the communists after the war. He'd fought with the wrong *partigiani*, there was a settling of accounts. There are still people, leftist people in Vicenza, who call him a *disgraziato*.

Here they were called *Rexists*, he said. A lot of people were *Rexists*.

Would you have been one, 'Enning?

Why ma'am, I'm just a po' old boy from Oklahoma…

I'm serious.

After all the history, it's easy to say no I wouldn't have. Far too easy.

How far is it to dinner?

Coming up. Anyway, my story's about done. When this part of

the world was liberated—in September 1944, after the famous battle of the Ardennes, where that American general said "Nuts!" when told to surrender—there was the usual purge. The men were shot, the women had their heads shaved. You've seen pictures.

Che barbaro!

Now here is the odd thing. The one thread that's out of place. And it has to do with time. Revenge is usually quick. Emotions get spent. But nearly a year went by before Emma H. was killed. Most of that bad stuff was over. Yet the men who later shot her took her away in a car and she was never seen again.

She said, Such things happened in Italy, too.

I know the names of the men. I know the names of three men. Here is my problem. The old lady, who is Emma's aunt, says she *knows* there were four. Now why would she invent a fourth if there wasn't one?

What difference does it make after so long?

Was she killed or was she executed? That's a difference. I would like to know more. You've seen those villages. Living with the Germans can't have been easy. And as for being *with* them, for a girl like Emma…? He left that hanging in the air.

Women are practical. Even very beautiful and young women like Ludi.

To be discussed over dinner, she said. She leaned back on her leather seat and closed her eyes. In her half-dreaming state in the delicious warmth of the car she composed a letter to friends in Vicenza, telling them how sensible and reliable Henning was. With Henning one felt *safe*.

Chapter two

Mevrouw Kerkevelde, *Tante* Berthe, knew she was not the most popular client of the *cabinet* Conincq, as it had once been known, where in Belgium, as in France, notaries call their practices 'cabinets'. For years, old Conincq had husbanded her father's money and then her brother's money and her sister's money and then hers when they were all dead. He had, however, tedious principles and a fetish for France which, considering French business practices—so delicately dishonest, she thought—was a bit rum. Naturally, during the war Conincq had disapproved of her and her business practices. A lot of people had. But they were poor and she was rich.

On the other hand, Conincq had been of real service to Emma, so her three chief interests—money, herself and Emma—had been well looked after. The firm no doubt had other wealthy clients, but none with the Kerkevelde tradition.

The old man had continued to disapprove of her after the war and he had—outrageously, she thought—suggested that Emma's death was in some way related to her affairs. One person trading with the enemy can be an accident or the result of a strong personality like yours, he'd said, but two?

She had always been decisive, so when Conincq had announced his retirement, it became no more than logical to use her money to buy the *cabinet* and put Jacques Coquin in charge. As it had been suitable for her—and prudent—to move from Liège to Mechelen when she came back from the long cruise she had taken after the so-called 'Liberation'. There had still been, after all, a number of matters to settle. Not least among them *l'heritage*, Emma's money. And the tedious business of fighting off communist troublemakers.

Coquin was entirely *her* man. He was useful and clever, but completely out of place in the staid, bourgeois culture of Liège. He was fifty-something. He leered. His little, plump body was meticulously maintained, rubbed, polished. He would have done a lot better, she thought, staying back in the Lebanon where his long eyelashes, melting black eyes, and cupid-bow lips would have been a distinct advantage.

And now he had become greedy. In the most deplorable, vulgar way. That is, he not only leered, he importuned. He wanted not just to handle her money but—so he regularly said—also to handle her, this while also making advances on her knee. At her age—she was at least twenty years older than he—how was she to cope with his often hinted-at desire for her body?

Berthe was no fool. She looked at herself, unstayed, and yes, she might be comforting, warm, smart, but especially she was rich. No doubt that was the attraction. But was her body even remotely interesting? Were she a man, would she be interested in Berthe Kerkevelde? Certainly not.

Despite his drawbacks, she had stuck with Coquin: in part because she was stubborn and in part because she thought he was close to ending an interminable law suit about a shoe factory she had owned and that had been hugely profitable during the war. It must have shod, she thought, a good part of the Wehrmacht. It was this little blemish in her affairs, as well as her general black-market affluence, that had led old Conincq to be so lofty and *moral*. And morality, she had discovered, was persistent and tenacious. Men! she thought. It was men who had a lock on such absurd abstractions. No woman had complained. Women knew that morality was a commodity like any other.

But at the end of the war it had all been too much for her. She'd gone off on a long trip to avoid scandal and, ashore one night, she'd met Coquin. Who also had certain aspects of his past to conceal.

What had she done to deserve all the attacks on her? She'd supplied shoes. What did it matter that they went on French feet or German? She was practicing her trade. That's what her father had said life was all about; *Arbeid*, work—that solid, irreproachable Flemish value—and she'd run the factory, bought the hides, found the rubber substitutes, organized the workers and run the canteen which had given her staff, mainly women, at least one decent meal a day. For this, the city council in Liège, freshly 'liberated' and mostly socialist or communist (she didn't see much difference between the two), had threatened her with a trial *in absentia*. And still revived the question regularly.

Now Coquin had called her for instructions, saying he had an appointment for the next day with Mr. Forsell, and she concluded—ridding herself of the anger that these preposterous accusations always raised in her—that the sneer in his voice was really very simple to explain. He was peeved. Jealous.

But *Mevrouw*, he would say, we have excellent and discreet people who have worked with this firm for years (and haven't done much for me or for Emma, she wanted to say). Just who *is* this gentleman you wish to employ? I must say, I am most disappointed. Of course, if you do not trust me with your affairs, then…

He could be very tedious and defensive, she thought. Not at all like old M. Conincq, who had been so thoughtful about Emma. *Too* thoughtful.

To Coquin, she said that she had nothing to add to the instructions she had already given regarding Mr. Forsell. Mr. Forsell would do very nicely, was her view, his great advantage being—which M. Coquin failed to see—that he wasn't local. He would come in, she hoped, and when he had finished, he would go away. It was much neater and preferable that way. It was always better not to let one's adversaries know too much about one, for knowledge was something that people could use.

For the same reason, she had not revealed much of what she truly felt about poor Emma in the original letter she had written to Mr. Forsell.

No, she was a cautious woman of the old school. Feelings were complex and often divided. And best kept to oneself.

At first, she'd done all she could for her dead sister's child: a ten-year-old of startling, icy beauty, whose every move had been away from her and into herself, into whatever impenetrable feelings she had. In her silent, obstinate, ever-so-pious way, the girl had always opposed everything, hadn't she? Emma and her music and her books and her learning (What sort of a monster had her sister and her husband created?), with her piety, her insistence on Catholicism when no one else in the family was anything but Dutch Reformed, her longish, sloping nose up in the air, that sort of slithery shyness which concealed a ferocious determination. A true Kerkevelde in that.

She'd been on board her ship near Lebanon when news of Emma's death reached her—a tiny paragraph in the ship's newspaper, brief murmurs of sympathy from the Captain at whose table she'd been seated—but the news hadn't surprised her. The child was a radical, and judging by her few friends, maybe even a Nazi.

When she thought of the things Emma had done during the war—not to speak of the things Emma had done that she knew nothing about—they only reinforced her view that all had not been well with the girl.

On the other hand, Tante Berthe was honest enough with herself to realize she did not know the whole story and as she grew older she felt she could not lie down and go to sleep—in the final sense, die—until she did know the truth. One way or another. Also she had one or two things on her conscience: things she might have done and hadn't.

How and why Emma had died, what had happened to her

I.I. Magdalen

money, what her life during the war and after had really been like. Hence Henning Forsell.

As she said to Coquin, telling him to give Mr. Forsell whatever help he needed, she just had a hunch about the American.

What was it, this hunch? Coquin wanted to know, beating about the bush as usual.

A quality of *listening*, she said.

He, of course, did not get the dig.

Chapter three

To be attracted to a girl who's been dead for twice the number of years than she'd been alive? That was a curious thing, thought Ludi, who not for the first time was coming to terms with the odd man she'd married.

For instance, in the three months they'd been married, she'd learned that Henning had no apparent home—at least not one she could determine. There was no place they went to that seemed to be it. Wherever they were, apartments or houses were effortlessly available to them, sometimes with resident servants. Henning took care of all the details and always had plenty of time to blend in with the surroundings. In London, or Rome, or Berlin, or Lisbon, he seemed at home. He knew the local food, what one 'did', the language, and, often enough, interesting people who turned up in the restaurants where they ate and seemed to like him greatly. She admired the fact that they liked him without his making any effort to be liked.

She giggled at what her Vicentine friends had said about him. The strong silent type. No, not quite. The Deep Thinker. Or, I wouldn't want to play poker against him. Well, some of that. Distracted? The absent-minded professor? Sometimes. A fair man? Not always. He's lots of different people, she wrote on their hotel stationery, and now I'm married to all of them. Who'd have thought it?

Now he said he'd found a lovely apartment on the Ile Saint Louis in Paris, Quai aux Fleurs. She was to go there and shop until she dropped, wander around, go see the Balthus paintings at the Pierre Matisse Gallery (he'd arranged that). He would join her in a few days.

This was because of that damned Emma H.

He said the logical place to start was with the men who had taken part in the execution. Old men now. That was why he had to stay behind in Liège a few more days.

He didn't think it necessary to tell Ludi what he had picked up on as he re-read Berthe's letter. That two of the men who came in the car to fetch her for her 'trial' hadn't the guts to do such a thing, one because he was too Catholic and too intellectual to act, the other because there was no real profit in it for him. But the third, she said—the third and the fourth—watch out for them. She didn't know who the fourth man was, only that he'd been present. The third was an ex-Hungarian communist, and *he* had every reason to act.

That stuck in his head.

Instead, he explained that all three of the identified men had been in the Resistance, though each of them in a different part. Two of them are not insignificant men. You see, you could make a career out of being a *Resistant*, it's like being vouched for. Whereas the old woman no longer counted for much. Like Emma, she was on *the wrong side*.

She pouted. She said, I think I hate this Emma.

What could Henning answer? This was what he did. True, this was the first time someone had asked him to find something out. Usually it was his own curiosity that got him pulling up stakes for strange places and odd people. The old woman had specifically said she'd read his last book. Of course, she'd said, I know I can't interest you with money. But with perplexity? To that you seem to respond.

Yes, he did. And recognized she was a sharp lady.

I.I. Magdalen

Thus when he'd taken Ludi off to the central station, he went on a crisp walk around. He liked what he saw. Growing up in a dry place, he had a real liking for broad, sluggish rivers. The Meuse, the Danube, the Vistula, the Mississippi.

His lunch meeting with M. Coquin had gone unexpectedly smoothly. The three men were alive, they were around. He said he'd arranged for Mr. Forsell to see the first one that very evening, though he must not expect that their stories would vary greatly from those produced in 1945. Nor should he expect, Coquin said rather cynically, that their memories would have greatly improved.

Oh that's all right, Henning said. I just like to have a clear picture in my mind. You know, the place, the time of day, I suppose how people felt at the time, about Emma, about the Germans.

Well, M. Coquin answered, Nous Taad is just the man for you, then. He's always been in the thick of things locally, though he's not really from here. He was a Hollander who worked in Germany, then a farmer until he joined the resistance. Which is probably where he met up with Tamas Kekes. Who by the way was a Communist. That was one way you could survive the war and get food.

And what is M. Taad now?

A businessman, M. Coquin answered. And a client, he added modestly.

What sort of business might that be?

Mostly transport. But a lot of things, really.

Henning thought that vague, but said nothing.

Taad is thinking of running for deputy.

Yes, I've heard of him, said Henning, who knew a good part of the Taad dossier from Brussels. Why should he be willing to talk to me and not, say, to Mme. Kerkevelde?

M. Coquin replied that it wasn't his business to pry, but he suspected the reason might be political.

You mean the investigations into Mme. Kerkevelde's businesses in 1947 and 1948?

M. Coquin looked surprised. He did not like underestimating his opponents. Even less so when they were American, and thus by definition backward about history. But he said that yes, that might have been a problem. Or *the* problem.

But the investigations were never concluded, said Henning. Or so I'm told. Is that right?

Times had changed, answered M. Coquin. Times always change.

Henning pressed him. He said, But if we know that Emma H was a collaborator, wouldn't Mme. Kerkevelde also qualify?

M. Coquin spread his expressive hands, palms up, on the snowy white cloth of their table: business, he said, was in a different category. Which made Henning wonder all sorts of things about the sleek notary, for in his own experience there were only two real reasons why otherwise estimable men were led to commit murder: money and power.

Henning said, One last thing. Would Emma have been a rich girl if she had lived?

She was a rich girl, M. Coquin answered. Even before she died.

Rich how?

Rich rich. She was an only child. And obviously she would have inherited from her aunt. Rich enough to do as she pleased. Rich enough to make a superb marriage. Rich enough to make lavish presents, some of them highly unsuitable. To indulge her caprices.

Henning duly noted the distaste. Had Berthe Kerkevelde shared Coquin's view? He said, I assume that Emma's money was handled by her aunt—at least at first.

Never! It was kept tight as a drum. M. Conincq, whose *cabinet* I bought, handled all her affairs. Hers was the only account he took with him when he retired.

Why would he do that?

He felt responsible for her? It could be that, the notary said, leaving a lot of room for the doubt in his mind.

Pardon my being so dense about Belgian law, but when Emma died, surely the money passed to her estate?

It may have been confiscated by the state. I do not know. You should ask M. Conincq.

Hard to image that neither you nor your client, Emma's aunt, would have fought that. If not for Emma's sake, then for your own.

That is an insinuation, M. Forsell, which I do not appreciate. Nor would Mme. Kerkevelde, who is a rich woman in her own right.

The rich people I know like to get richer.

It would have amused Ludi to know that Henning thought of this as a lunch that went smoothly. But in Henning's view it had. The girl was capricious, she was headstrong, she strewed money about (a lot of people would have been interested in that), but unlike her aunt, Emma had not been able to use her money to escape her fate at the end of the war. Why would that be? Certainly not because the locals were above being suborned. Because there wasn't any money left? Because she couldn't get to it? Because someone had already taken it?

On his way back to his hotel before meeting Nous Taad, Henning stopped by the police *commissariat*. His Brussels bank had given him a name, *Commissaire* Masquelier. The *Commissaire*—a man with thin hair and the mottled cheeks and nose of a habitual drinker—received him with elaborate courtesy, which told Henning the Bank had laid it on thick for him.

He said that absolutely anything he could do for Monsieur Forsell would cause him the most exquisite pleasure. Proudly, he pulled a large envelope from his drawer and presented it to Henning. He said, These are copies of a few documents I found in the files.

Henning thanked him. He said, I would willingly stay a while—there is so much you could tell me about the town and its citizens—but I am due to see Mr. Nous Taad at his office in a brief while. Is there anything I should know about him?

The *Commissaire* looked guilelessly across his desk at Henning and said, One of our Leading Citizens. The quotation marks Henning

Emma H.

heard around 'Leading Citizens' made it plain that Masquelier had little use for such people.

Thank you, *Commissaire*, said Henning. I am warned.

The *Commissaire*, Henning also thought, would be just about the same age as the others. Pushing retirement with not a few secrets in his own back pocket.

Chapter four

Nous Taad—aka Vieuxtemps in the Resistance—was not exactly pleased to have a meeting scheduled with an American called Henning Forsell. Americans were a footloose, dangerous, highly moralizing race. Like the citizens of any empire, they had seized the high ground of self-righteousness. Secretly (but openly with his war-time buddies) he disliked them for that, and for their lack of savoir-faire, their wealth, their greed in business, their pink-cheeked and big-thighed luxury. The war—that cardinal event in his lifetime—had not been fought on their soil, no; it had been fought on his own adopted turf, right here.

Way down inside Nous was afraid of them. Because they had power.

The German occupation had come in 1940 while he had been doing his futile military service. They had been overrun in a few days and he had shed his uniform and biked back home to the farm ten kilometers outside town where, as the sole support of his ailing mother and because agricultural production was important for the Reich, he had kept his head down and been untroubled until the allied invasion of Normandy. By then, in a big city like Liège, it had become necessary to make choices: collaboration by default, or joining the resistance.

Well, the local *maquis* was a patchy cross-border affair and riven by politics. You could fight with the conservative Walloon (French-speaking) group headed by the elegant and abstract Bernard Pons. Or you could join in with Tamas Kekes and the communists. Nous wasn't elegant and he wasn't interested in the Hungarian's sooty, drab, doctrinaire socialism. In fact, he feared him even more than he did the Germans, which was why he had retained many of the documents of the day. Just in case. He had proofs and had let it be known he had proofs. That was why the local Reds would not oppose him in the elections; and he, in return, saw to it they got their share of his business.

In the same spirit, he had remained independent of any grouping and had done his bit with exemplary self-interest. When it finally seemed the Germans were going to lose the war, he understood it would be those who had distinguished themselves fighting against the occupiers who would rise to the top. He had distinguished himself and he had been rewarded.

On to the American then, whom he saw in the outer office speaking to Nicole (Mlle. Pascal). Utterly relaxed. A large man, vaguely blond.

Americans all seemed inordinately large: like their cars, their women, their steaks.

Fundamentally he felt he was right. It would have been unwise to refuse to see this American. After all, though he had a good deal to hide, he had nothing on his conscience. (He allowed himself a little smile—of the kind that made Mlle. Pascale elaborate, in bed, on his 'boyish charm'—at the thought of his conscience.) Furthermore, as his good friend the *Commissaire,* Masquelier, had confided earlier, this was an American with friends in high places, and in politics such people can only do you harm if you do not humor them in their little whims, such as their interest in the events of thirty-eight years ago.

Yet again, he thought, glancing at the illuminated sign on the outside of his building, "Bouwerk Taad", what could an American possibly do to him?

He'd seen them come through town on their conquering way (what were swollen rivers to men who assembled bridges on the spot?)—all of them as startlingly big and solid as this American was—and compared their inexhaustible supplies of cigarettes to the wretched two packs a month most people (although not he) got. He had also compared the ersatz coffee they'd served in those days in what were now once again big, profitable cafés, to their cheerful and endless supply of the real thing. He had seen them take the local women—obviously, not girls of breeding like Emma H., but big raw-boned proper women with powerful pelvises and the shoulders of oxen. The Amis had come, the Amis had gone. The *Boches* had been here to the bitter end, but they too straggled off one by one, and could be picked off at random.

No, this American would also go away. With Americans you needed to baffle by sincerity. Could he summon it up? For instance say: But *cher Monsieur*, we three may have acted together at one time but we do not have to love one another! We acted under different constraints and with different aims.

He suddenly thought of something else that the *Commissaire* had told him, that this Mr. Forsell not only spoke perfect French but was sharpish in Flemish too. Of how many Americans could you say that? That is, normal Americans. And he has money, Masquelier had finished up triumphantly. I would judge, lots of money.

Of course he had taken the precaution of calling both Tamas and Bernard: Tamas at his party headquarters which he hardly ever left—despite his city job—and Bernard at the café where he kept his napkin and ring and ate every day at twelve sharp.

It had taken both men a little time to grasp what he was talking about. But all that's so long ago, Bernard had said with irritation—perhaps his main course had just arrived and he didn't want it to get cold—while Tamas, with that bitter, guttural voice of his, had grasped the nettle right away: It's that old Kerkevelde bitch. She's the one that should have been taken care of.

Nous replied calmly that she'd been out of reach at the time. Though of course he had to assume there were presumably party members in the Near East who would have welcomed the liquidation of a bourgeoisie who sold shoes to the Germans. Little cur, he thought. An operator by proxy, a traitor by trade.

Don't do politics with me, Tamas said. Take care of this American. Watch out. They have a mania for re-opening the past, things that are better forgotten.

As for Bernard, he said in that lofty way he had, If you find him difficult, send him to me. Keep Kekes out of it. We've always agreed on that.

Finally, sure that he knew how to handle this American, he pushed the buzzer on his desk and Mlle. Pascal answered. He said, The American gentleman has arrived?

Yes, M. Taad.

Then send him in. Bring us the usual.

In effect, Henning said, sitting down in the big leather chair across from him, he didn't know a great deal about Miss Hoofrad, and what little he did know was contradictory. He hoped M. Taad might be able to help him.

Of course, of course, said Nous genially. It was a very long time ago and—well, naturally—he didn't know much about the poor, misguided girl. Our paths didn't cross, he said. You must have an expression for it in America. When two people come from different backgrounds...

The other side of the tracks, Henning said. One lived on the right or the wrong side of where the train went through.

Precisely, said Nous. The girl was from what we used to call a 'good family'. I was of a more modest family, a farm family. It's funny now, but back then we didn't even think of meeting girls like Emma. We might see them, of course: in the streets, biking to school, in the windows of restaurants. You understand, they had a freedom we did not have. Nor was her family from here, I understand. They were from Maastricht, I think.

I.I. Magdalen

Nonetheless you had a good deal of information about her.

About the war? About her activities, what she did? Yes, there was plenty of proof. Witnesses and so on.

But nothing official.

Those were confusing times, Taad explained patiently. You can consider yourselves lucky. Your country was not occupied.

My family comes from Oklahoma. That is Osage country. It was taken over by settlers.

Nous looked more closely at Henning. He didn't look like a redskin. Maybe the aquiline nose, the cheekbones, but surely not the blue eyes and that rather colorless hair. So he assumed Henning's family was among the settlers. Evidently that is not the same thing, he said. Perhaps yours was more or less an empty country. Belgium is a very full country. As is Holland, where my family came from.

Empty? Not to the Osage.

Well, it was different here. We had a military occupation. The *Boches*, the Germans, were here for four years. Four years. Imagine.

While Nous let that sink in, Henning had a chance to size up his man. Fleshy and sanguine, he concluded. Skin that was meant to show youth, vigor, and health, but actually looked as if it had been smeared with facial cream, the whole face shining but for a prominent mole an inch below Taad's left eye. Late fifties or more, and self-important; an office arranged in such a way as to indicate furious activity and lack of time, papers unpinned, letters skewered into envelopes, the desk-top littered with paper-clips and bungled staples.

Two things were evident to Henning: first that the war had been no real hardship to Nous Taad (Henning had seen real suffering still etched on French, Italian, Russian, and even German faces) and second, that the man was perfectly capable of cold-blooded murder if it suited his purpose.

But even then Henning hadn't thought that Emma had been murdered *in cold blood*. No, she had been killed out of hatred and some sort of perverse envy.

Henning liked to be taken for a plain man. His face expressed perplexity at those four years, as if he had the greatest difficulty imagining what they might have been like. He said tentatively, I suppose there were hard feelings afterward. Some went one way, others went another.

It couldn't have been put more blandly. It was an invitation, which Nous accepted gratefully, to polish his own image. Of course (there it was again, the self-evident nature of what had happened, the past all neatly locked into place) you should not overestimate the strength of the Resistance. We were really very few. The older people here…Well, they'd been occupied for four years during the '14–'18 war too. They were not indifferent but they had to go on living. You could call them passive, though many of them were ashamed; to have been so easily beaten; by the attitude of the King, who fled; by their army, which dropped its weapons and ran.

Weakness is not a reason for the execution of a nineteen-year-old girl so long after the war was over. Others had stronger convictions.

Oh, very few. On either side.

Enough to have a small war of their own.

A shadow passed across Taad's face. He said, I wouldn't put it that way. We—that is, those who continued to fight the Germans—were simply a part of the larger war that was engulfing the whole world.

Whereas the others, like Emma, were in a small war of their own?

If your Indians joined up with the settlers and shot their own kind, would that be a 'small war'?

I meant their convictions: that the Germans were right; that what the country needed was fascism, authority…

Eliminating the sick, the elderly, Jews, the handicapped, their political opponents, pastors who didn't conform.

I understand all that. I'm puzzled that someone from Emma's background should have such beliefs. She was very young and she was a woman, a girl.

They're the worst kind. Women can be much more cruel than men.

She was cruel?

Unrepentant is how I would put it. Convinced that she was right.

So she had a chance to defend herself? There was a trial of some kind? At which she could state her beliefs?

There must have been. Our orders were clear.

That late? But you don't know of one. A trial, I mean.

Look, at the end of the war all sorts of unpleasant things happened. People accused each other, out of spite, out of resentment pent up for all that time.

Like the 'excesses' of the Bolsheviks, I take it.

Taad wasn't sure whether the remark was ironical in intent or merely a statement of fact. So he said, There are things of which people are not proud today: shaving the heads of women who slept with the *Boches*, some settling of accounts.

But that soon stopped.

Yes.

But six months later, Emma was executed. There was no more confusion.

People surfaced, people came back thinking they were safe, witnesses appeared who had been silent before.

I take it then there was a trial. And that you took part in it. And that you are not amongst those who felt uneasy about what you'd done.

I did my duty. I followed orders.

Yes, I see. I won't ask you *whose* orders.

Kekes' orders, Nous said. Not mine.

It doesn't really matter. That will all come out, I'm sure. One last thing. What was Emma's behavior at the end, when you took her away? I take it she knew she was going to be shot? Did she struggle, complain, demand, shout obscenities…I don't know, whatever people do when they know they're going to die and don't think they should. What does a nineteen-year-old feel at such a time?

I've said it already, Monsieur Henning. Unrepentant. Emma Hoofrad was unrepentant. She despised us.

Emma H.

Back at his hotel Henning called Ludi as he'd promised. She sounded happy and unaffected. Given the address, she said, what could I do but fill the apartment with flowers! But they look at me sadly, wondering when you'll arrive. You know, I never liked Paris when I used to come here as a schoolgirl to learn French. The people were stuck-up and unpleasant. But now that I live here, it seems it's all mine. I walk all over it for miles. I take the Metro to places I don't know. Why aren't you here to enjoy it with me? Though obviously, as with everything else, you probably know it all by heart. Haven't you finished with that girl yet?

He laughed at the idea of this girl, this child-woman, filling their apartment with flowers—it was so like her!—and longed to be there with her.

He said, however, no, not yet. The only thing that is clear to me is that everyone wants to forget about her. It's as though she never really existed. Or she's not a girl but some sort of spirit. Yet she was only a year or two younger than you! You've seen her picture. Can you imagine her not existing? People who knew her not remembering her? Even those who had to point a gun at her and shoot her?

There followed many endearments. And in Henning, a kind of suppressed fury. One could not blame the shooting of a nineteen-year-old girl, a beauty with a lofty brow, on history, on circumstances, on confusion, on animosity, on war, on any other abstraction. Crimes were committed by human beings against other human beings. Even a suicide, like his father's, was a crime against a human being by a human being: against himself and against those he deprived of himself, his wife, who had loved her husband, and his son, who had abruptly ceased to know or understand him.

Chapter five

It struck Henning during the night that he had probably made a mistake plunging in like that with Nous Taad, asking him questions about Emma which, even had he been able to answer, he would have chosen not to. In his clumsy, honest, Oklahoma way (not that Oklahoma was especially honest, but it was the way Oklahomans saw themselves) he had given Nous the opportunity to warn his two *maquis* buddies—if that was all they were—Pons and Kekes. Sitting in his duck blind, Henning had inadvertently flushed out the game. He had not made a good start, and that was mistake Number One.

He should have seen that for the practical, energetic, let's look to the future Taad, ('Of course') Emma was a part of the past, a wartime incident, one of many—some tragic, others simply ludicrous. That's what he would have said: in or out of his office, as political candidate or businessman. Those were tough times. Fair enough, we're none of us perfect, in war human life isn't valued as it is in times of peace. Many young people disappeared and their elders (their parents, teachers, and mentors) were in no position to ask questions.

Many millions had 'disappeared' in this cruel century and only long afterwards were questions asked.

So what had Henning expected of Taad? That he stand defiantly on the truth? Thirty-eight years after the event he might indeed have had some second thoughts about Emma's death, but how could he say so without denying a part of what had been himself? And pushing Nous into positions that could put him into danger—for Henning was already pretty certain that Nous Taad had not been a prime mover. No, a man of convenience. And one who would be well armed against the past.

Well, he wasn't back home on the range—where seldom was heard a discouraging word—he was in a strange, rainy, and recent country with a delicate, even difficult texture about which he knew too damn little.

Start with the victim, he said to himself. Someone (*Mevrouw* Kerkevelde) had described Emma as a 'remarkable' pianist. That at least gave the girl, who had barely lived, an attribute of some kind. That is, Emma had been something before she became another person, the one who'd done whatever it was she was accused of and paid for it with her life. That was where he should have started.

She would have studied. Where? In Maastricht where her family came from, in Mechelen where she'd lived with her Tante Berthe Kerkevelde, or here in Liège where she had turned up in early adolescence?

He imagined her hands, long, as they were in the Flemish paintings that she resembled, resting on the keyboard before attacking one of the great Beethoven sonatas.

There was something still about the girl that he couldn't quite put his finger on. Still like lake-water. The stillness of repose or contemplation. Or, as in the Vermeer paintings Henning loved, of acceptance. Yet the photograph he'd seen (Aged what? Fifteen?) was artless, the sort of studio shot that got taken on First Communion, on graduation—Emma in a studio, her hands clasped before her, wearing a dress with a scalloped collar and a gold chain around her slender neck with a cross or a scapular.

Stillness. And a great beauty.

The world was full of pretty girls, and some beauties; great beauties were very rare and he felt lucky to have seen one, even if she was dead.

Mind you, his Ludi was a beauty, risen fresh and curly from some Tyrrhenian sea, but she wasn't a great beauty.

Truly great beauties were young or very young. They were unforgettable and also unattainable. Usually they weren't conscious of their beauty, because it didn't consist of the way nature had put all the parts together—eyes, neck, shape, skin, lips, mouth, ears, hair, brow—but in something moral and distant, unaware and utterly exceptional.

Even from the memory of a photograph. Henning had no doubt that Emma H. had been one of the truly great beauties. And if you've seen one, like everyone else, you have this terrible knowledge: that sort of beauty does not last. It hadn't.

Three or four men had found her out, tried her, judged her, driven her away, and killed her up in the hills. They must have had a good long look at her. How could they have shot her? Spoiled that body, violated that stillness? At Emma's age, how important a collaborator could she have been? To produce such a belated and terrible revenge? His last thought that night was that in all walks of life, as in all extreme acts, like killing, reasons overlapped reasons; apparent motives concealed deeper, hidden motives; explanations hid lies. And weren't love and jealousy as good prompts to murder as having backed the 'wrong side'?

*

Who had given Emma master classes just before the war? His name was Andrzej Niemczyk and he was Polish. A harassed and anxious secretary at the Conservatory found Henning the class lists for the late 1930s.

To be admitted at that age (Let me see, born in November 1925…Why she was barely fourteen!) she'd have to have been very talented. It was long before her time. And then there was the war.

And her teachers? Henning asked patiently.

The secretary had one of those French mouths: thin and very accurately delineated lips, aggressive like a purposeful fish.

All it says in her file is that she was having private lessons.

She handed him a worn sheet—apparently in Emma's hand—asking to be allowed to work with a Polish pianist she had met over that summer of 1939.

The secretary disapproved. The Pole wasn't a member of the regular faculty. It wouldn't normally be allowed.

Nothing about him? Henning asked.

His name, Niemczyk. Still alive, Monsieur? Still here? There was a war, you know. And he was Polish. It is very unlikely. She crossed thin arms on a flat chest and said, *Bon Dieu*! This is not a police inquiry?

He reassured her.

Yes, she said. But why?

A legal question. I assure you it is important, or I would not waste your valuable time. An address? Something?

It is for her good?

She is dead, Madame.

Oh.

She leafed through the slender file.

Here, she said. It does not say whose address it is. Maybe it is his? Or hers?

A forty-year-old address was better than nothing. It was out of town. Down-river.

A half-day went by finding a telephone number. Way out of town, down-river. The lady who answered sounded old and indignant in equal parts. He must be mad to think she could know where her tenant had gone so many years ago. But yes, she remembered him.

The remark she then made struck Henning as strange: if, that is, the pianist had made no impression on her. She said, He was a rather pretty man. A young girl used to come out and see him.

A 'pretty' man?

I must have his address somewhere. He asked me to send on

his mail. Polish newspapers. But of course there was the war. You've looked in the *annuaire*?

Yes. There were no Niemczyks listed in the phone book.

A day later—landladies being nothing if not meticulous record-keepers—she called Henning back with an address.

She said, There's a lot of music of his down in the cellar. Tell him I'd be glad to get rid of it.

The concierge in Henning's hotel said he had no idea where the address was. He called the post office for Henning.

You can't drive there, he said. It's up the Meuse toward Tilleur, a part heavily damaged by the v-2's during the war. They say no one lives there now, but I think that only means they don't deliver letters there.

So Henning went to the post office and wrote a telegram and the next day got a call from the pianist.

You'll understand this wasn't a promising beginning, he told Ludi on the phone that night. It gets worse.

The Pole sounded as though he'd never used a telephone in his life. His voice was indistinct, hoarse and accented. When, after much to'ing and fro'ing (I don't see many people, It's been so many years, Can't everyone just leave me alone?) Henning explained why he wanted to see him and mentioned the name Emma, there was a long silence: and finally a sigh.

A-a-h. This was followed by another long silence, and then, Her. I knew she wouldn't leave me alone.

Dead, how could she bother him? He put it down to Andrzej's imperfect French and eventually extracted an appointment to meet him four days later. The Pole chose the place (a bar?) which he called 'Madame Elizabeth's'. He said it was the only place he ever went, and gave elaborate directions.

Henning made fun of this conversation when talking to Ludi, but on reflection it had not been funny at all. On the contrary, it had been deeply sad. He'd felt as though he'd been talking to a man who had long ago pulled the plug on his own life.

If you want to know what it was like, imagine yourself talking to a dog or cat that's gone outside somewhere to die. They don't want to know. You can't comfort them. The last thing they would consult is memory. I mean, what use is memory when you're about to die?

And being around Niemczyk was hard too. It was like walking through slurry: bits and pieces of solid matter in a liquid mess. What did Henning really remember from that Saturday? Not much. A general impression of having lifted the corner of a page or parted a curtain and having seen something totally alien. And desperate.

Elizabeth's was a kind of bar. It had smoke-sodden walls and posters of pre-war bike races. He could summon up a smell of salt fish, and also the proprietress's slab face and long chin. What had struck him most was the disorder of Andrzej's mind, his streaky, gray hair plastered to his narrow skull which reminded him of the elderly, bald waiters of Eastern Europe and remote cafés in Argentina; the stubble scattered in patches from chin to cheek, the very large nose that occupied fully half his face; the drinker's mottled cheeks. Pretty?

To understand this man, Henning said, he had to put himself in the Pole's place.

Believe me, you wouldn't want to be there. To be sixty-something, living alone, scared of life, drinking too much?

No, it was obvious something had gone wrong with Niemczyk's life. Why leave Poland in the mid-1930s? The man wasn't Jewish.

I just couldn't work him out.

He'd tried hard, but the confusion was too great. Confusion in his own mind, which didn't want to be dragged down into Slav melancholy but would rather—isn't this always the case at thirty-three?—embrace the future and the girl he'd just married; confusion in Andrzej's, which had never had a steady focus or something to head *toward*.

For instance, when Henning led him back to those years and then the war, it seemed Andrzej didn't really remember the war, neither its end nor its beginning. He accepted the drinks Henning offered, his watery blue eyes wandered about the dark room, but he shuffled around that subject; he shuffled around every subject Henning brought up. Didn't remember, didn't want to remember. His

I.1. Magdalen

eyes never changed expression. They didn't look inward, they didn't look outward. They neither registered nor communicated.

Again, putting himself in the Pole's place, Henning managed just this little fragment of understanding: that nothing's happened to me for years and years, I've forgotten everything I ever knew, and anyone who knew me has forgotten all about me. So suddenly, out of the blue, a stranger's turned up and invited me to have a drink. Who the stranger is, well, that's not important. The drink is important.

Taking it that far was no problem for Henning. He knew all about safe places: the gulch by the northwest hundred, where his old man kept the original leases the Tribal Council handed him, the tin box with letters from the past, the confident stare with which his Pa kept anyone from asking questions they shouldn't.

*

Everyone has safe places. Elizabeth's was Andrzej's. By Henning's guess, had long been. Here he was known, more or less. With his own kind: old Poles and a few of their sons who sat there playing cards and drinking in a welter of languages and dialects, none of them French or Flemish.

The war? Niemczyk said finally. There must have been a war if an American tells me so.

From anyone else that would have been a joke.

More time went by. Then the Pole made a brief excursus into music. It wasn't connected to the war, but it was to Emma. One time, he said, he had been very passionate about music.

When I am young.

Play me something, said Henning.

The Pole said he had given all that up years ago. But perhaps he hadn't. Maybe it was more a matter of indifference.

You can imagine, Henning said to Ludi, how much I would like to be able to say the man was a neglected genius, that his Chopin was like Warszowski's! But I was sure it wasn't. And probably never had been.

Nonetheless, with a stop first at the toilet that was outside the back door, Andrzej shambled over to an old upright in a corner and played a few mazurkas—indifferently. No one paid the slightest attention, which meant he did it often enough—if someone bought him a drink. Maybe sometimes better and sometimes even worse.

Then he came back and wanted another drink.

Maudlin, Henning said, in that Polish way. My reading was: he'd bungled his life or been bungled by life itself. He didn't care any more.

A few more drinks, a good many, and Andrzej was rambling on through the broken shards of his history. How he'd had to push his way—a miner's son from Silesia. It had been push and kick, kick and trample. He'd been sent to Warsaw by his parish priest on a scholarship. But at school he'd been surrounded by the fortunate children of the bourgeoisie, clever Jews, or aristocrats.

And so on, Henning said. You get the picture. I finally walked him home, he wheeling his rickety old bike unsteadily alongside me; a beret perched on his head. We must have looked like a pair of tramps leaning on one another, but I didn't think he'd make it otherwise.

And your girl? Ludi asked. Your beloved Emma?

I'm coming to that.

As he had, that Saturday. Along an overgrown, grassy path that ran alongside the canal, a tiny house, barely more than two rooms on either side of a low front door through which Henning had to duck. To his right there was a cot against one wall, with a grubby picture of the Virgin of Czestochowa pinned to the wallpaper. By the window was a table with a vodka bottle (almost empty) and a tin plate bearing a knife, fork, and spoon—nothing to cook on that Henning could see. On the other side, when Andrzej parted a flowered curtain hung on a string, there was another room with a tiny window, some shelves on the wall, and a single chair.

And there was the surprise: a full old Pleyel concert grand piano of fine-grained light walnut—an instrument for dreams, Henning thought and said.

The walk seemed to have brought the pianist briefly back to life. He grunted in the general direction of the piano and said: Out of tune. Sit down. You want to talk more? You've had enough of an old man?

And these? Henning said, picking up two photographs that stood on the dusty surface of the Pleyel.

Me.

The young Andrzej with a meager bouquet of flowers in his hand.

Oh, very beautiful our Andrzej was back then, Henning told Ludi. Or 'pretty' as his once-upon-a-time landlady had said. Tall, sensitive, the way certain Poles can be: long curly hair, long tapering fingers. An air of being too good for the things of this world. If he'd been a military man, like my friend Czapski who found us the apartment you're in, he'd have had long boots up to his thighs made of the supplest calf-leather. No Silesian miner's son, that's for sure. He wouldn't have lasted a minute.

Then what? she asked.

Then I kept looking at the picture. I knew there was a story there, because he'd kept that picture all these years.

Meanwhile, Niemczyk had turned surly again. He said, You don't want to sit down, I sit. If it was possible to slump on a hard chair, that was what he did: legs stretched out in dirty thick-waled corduroy, a faded blue workman's shirt open to straggly hair on his chest.

In Lodz, he said. In the hall of the Sokol, or Gymnastic Society. My debut. A disaster. I leave out whole bars. I don't care. I make mistakes on purpose in the Scriabin piece.

And the girl?

Pah! Just a schoolgirl. A second-year student.

What really happened, or part of what happened, came out a bit later. The schoolgirl had been appointed by the Sokol to present him the traditional bouquet at the end of the concert. But by then, bit by bit, and then *en masse*, the audience had gone. The schoolgirl didn't know what to do. In the end she had just dumped the bouquet in his hand and fled.

It had to do with humiliation, Henning understood. The worst kind was the kind you inflicted on yourself.

He held up the second photograph.
And this one?
That is Emma. You have a cigarette?
A younger Emma than the one Henning had seen, looking shyly away from the camera. She wore a fetching straw hat and a sailor blouse.

Henning handed him a cigarette and lit it for him. The pianist's hands shook as he cupped them around the flame.

There was a war, Andrzej said, studying the photograph, something stirring inside him. She gave me the picture, she came on a bicycle where I was without permission, because it is the day Hitler attacks Poland.

He said that though he looked at the photographs every day, this was the first time in years he had remembered the coincidence; that she'd given him that picture on the day the war broke out. I forget everything, he said. Now I remember I tell her Poland cannot possibly hold out. Poles will lose. They always lose.

She understood?

Of course she understands. She is fourteen, but she understands. She is full of life. She sees war, she knows what that means. She is a young girl who understands everything. She understands too much. For me at least.

I had many feelings when he said that, you can imagine, Henning said to Ludi. The way he pulled himself together, drew himself up out of that chair and went and stood next to the piano. A beautiful instrument by the way. In those surroundings! A hovel. Imagine! I thought: the piano is like his mind. The notes were all still there, but none of them fit or are ever played. I thought how slowly his days must crawl by. How he talked to no one. How did he pass his time? I asked him, and he said he didn't need time or heed time. He showed me an old chess problem from a local paper, white to mate in four moves. Sometimes I do that, he said.

And the piano? Ludi asked.

It was a gift from Emma. Then he stopped talking.

Henning remembered him as looking down at the chess problem. That might have been what time meant to him. That one day he might come up with a solution.

That's all? Ludi asked.

No. He said, She's dead you know.

That was when for the first time Henning got the impression the pianist had actually seen him, looked him in the eye. Then he added, looking away again, No, she's *really* dead, you know. You have to believe that. Dead to everyone.

For a long time after that—a good quarter-hour—Henning sat in the chair where the pianist had sat and Andrzej stood by the piano. Apparently with nothing going on in his mind. Or maybe it was reverie or fear. Or what Henning recognized in him: the perennial exile to whom nothing is as valuable as the place he has fled and to which he can't return. He might have been—in fact he had been—a terrible failure back there, but he was a failure here too. But whereas in Lodz or Warsaw or wherever there might have been a reason for his failure (panic, irresponsibility, refusal) there was no such reason here. It was as if he didn't exist at all, didn't care to, saw no way to do so.

In fact, Henning said to Ludi, he only said a few things more. One was that he was old and not well and I shouldn't take him seriously, and another was that no one had any right to know what Emma had meant to him.

That's it?

No, the last thing he said was, She wanted me, she wanted me so badly. That's when he stopped talking altogether.

Come to Paris, 'Enning, she said. You sound depressed yourself.

There could be something in it, you never know, do you. A fourteen-year-old and a Pole more than twice her age. That he was a failure doesn't mean that he couldn't have loved her, or that she loved him, the way adolescents do fall in love with their teachers, if that's what he was. There was music. I was quite sure Emma had played on that piano, often. By the way he ran his hand over the wood and perhaps desperately wanted to open it up and be able to play.

Maybe she was in love with him, however impossible it seems—for the music.

Ludi let that linger for a moment, then said: *Può darsi*. It's possible. Also that he fell in love with her, for *her* music.

From then to now is a long time to mourn.

You are not practical, 'Enning. It is perhaps because you are rich you don't think of such things…

He was distracted.

What things?

What he lives on. Your ghostly lover.

A pension?

You should check. No telephone, you say. No post-box. No cigarettes.

What the pianist had said about Emma had irrevocably changed Henning's view of her. That was what distracted him.

On Monday he got a postcard from Ludi. 'I think when you are working on these things you don't care about anyone or anything else. They are your secret life. I am as jealous as if you had a mistress. Come back quickly.'

He did as Ludi said. Checked. The whole strip of land—from Andrzej's house to Madame Elizabeth's bar, was Church land. There had once been a chapel there. Thanks to his Brussels friend, he learned that the Pole received a tiny allocation from the Belgian Government. He also had a post-office account on which quarterly payments were made and had been made ever since the war. They weren't a great sum but with interest—and considering they'd never been touched—the balance was substantial. The payments were made by a Church charity.

And not even a powerful Brussels bank, Henning's friend said, can find out about those.

Emma again? Henning wondered.

Chapter six

It was a Sunday, and raining. Nothing unusual about that, thought Kekes Tamas (the way Hungarians wrote it, surname first). There was a Sunday every week; it often rained. As he did every morning, he washed himself scrupulously in cold water from a basin in the room he rented by the week. He then washed his glasses, thick as fog-lights, with equal care, placed them on his short, sharp nose and ran his fingers through his thinning ginger hair. Finally, donning his blue work shirt to identify himself more closely with the laboring class, he realized he was in an unproductive and ugly frame of mind.

When he was like that, nothing good ever came of it. To prevail in the struggle against the bourgeoisie, one required the icy discipline of a Vladimir Ilyich, to whom nothing personal really mattered. One's class enemies were one's class enemies and that was that. Emotions didn't enter into it.

But they always did, didn't they? He deeply wished it wasn't so, but it was. And worse, this 'feeling' part of you was what people thought of as your 'good' side. In fact, it was the weak side. It was the side that put you at risk. And once Nous Taad had called him at his office, he felt at risk.

Yet if he'd had no feelings he wouldn't be at risk. That is, whatever he'd done for a reason, out of logic, had involved no feeling at all. It was necessary that it be done, it was done. Neither before, or after was he affected by any feeling about his actions. Logic gave him little choice and it seemed he was at that very point again.

He sometimes felt that if women didn't exist—by which he meant women who hadn't wiped out their essential femininity, their desire to attach themselves to another, their love of comfort and privacy, who hadn't become *Kameraden, compagnons*, people you could rely on as though they had no gender at all—then one could commit fully to what was really important in life. Which for him meant destroying so that rebuilding could take place.

But women did exist and he'd had a wife, Jeanne, and he'd loved her with a devotion that he found inexplicable and destructive. That had been a first weakness, a breach of the inner discipline that had kept him going. Logic had gone to the wind and he still ached for her.

It had been in a mid-winter when he'd more or less just arrived in Mechelen. And that only after several long, difficult journeys. He had found a room and registered to continue his engineering studies. He had just begun to find his way about the town whose circular shape and winding river had baffled him.

Struggling with his weak eyesight, he first noticed her at the damp, dark market. She was helping her mother sell vegetables at a stall. He found out later she was eighteen, but he'd seen her as much younger than that. Underdeveloped like a kid. She had straggly dirty blond hair and a long sloping nose.

His first thought had been that the child should have been sitting in a warm schoolroom, not wrapped up in sweaters under the rain.

She was obviously sick. Anyone could see that in her sloping shoulders and sunken chest. So that his first movement toward her had been one of recognition. She was like him. His second was of

I.I. Magdalen

pity rather than love. In a just world she would not be consumed by poverty and by what was eating away at her from inside.

Only when he started work for the city's public works department, and after many visits to the stall buying vegetables one at a time, did he first talk to her and learn her name, Jeanne. Then once, when her mother was talking to another customer and weighing several bunches of leeks, he asked the girl if she would come to an anti-fascist rally at which he would be speaking.

She didn't seem to understand what a rally was, or fascists, but she came. She stared at him from the front row while he spoke eloquently in his heavily accented French about his experiences with the dictatorship in Hungary. His weak blue eyes watered and he couldn't see her clearly, though he had arranged with a comrade that she should sit in the front row. His eyes watered again, making Jeanne into a vague shape, when three months later he asked her to marry him.

He asked her out of pity, out of a deep sense of the injustice of her life—you could also say out of political compassion.

It had been a marriage born in sorrow and ending in worse, in something like despair. He had been like someone on the banks of a swollen river, hanging on to Jeanne as, moment by moment, day by day, she slipped from his fingers.

For the second weakness (the first was to allow himself to love at all) lay in encouraging—as though there were any hope at all—her fortitude, her hope.

Aware of her frailty, she'd nonetheless wanted some happiness out of what was left of her life and, if possible, a child. No child came, but instead of allowing her to die (after all, what was one death more or less in those times?) he had protected her, done all the housework when she had taken to her bed, soothed her, warmed her and, having given up his studies, all he had in return was the privilege of watching her die on the operating table in the second year of the war, eighteen months after they had married.

The same doctor who brought him the news outside the operating room had said it all at her first consultation: There is nothing I can do for her.

Nevertheless, Tamas had argued, taken other opinions, and insisted on the operation. That way she would suffer less. That was the third weakness. In this life one should expect pain.

He had walked home from the hospital with a terrible anger in his heart: anger at the callousness of the doctor who said he couldn't do anything; anger at Jeanne; anger at the rosy-cheeked priest who aided and abetted and preached resignation to poor Jeanne; and harsher yet, the anger he'd felt crossing a group of laughing, healthy girls walking to their convent school. (One of them could easily have been Emma.)

When he thought back to those days there came back to him, like a pungent odor, the same terrible anger any man feels who is helpless before the inevitable, who is forever marked as a man apart, one who is never going to be as others, or share in their joys.

After Jeanne's death, he was not only alone, but knew he would always be alone and always living in one cheap room or another and working for a miserable wage while doing his political work—the only thing left that mattered and that he should never have left.

For a long time, the war left him unmoved. After Ribbentrop and Molotov got together to carve up Poland, the Germans were allies in the world revolution to come. Then, when the fatherland of the revolution was attacked, there was the occupation and moving from place to place, from one comrade to another.

Nothing had changed in his life. Even now, on this particular Sunday, there was the depression brought on by looking out the window (his was a back room) and seeing the rain drip in sheets from slate roofs or, if he looked down, at the rotting metal in the yard beneath—bikes and disused fencing, once-upon-a-time lawn mowers.

For all the years since that loss, he could think only one thing: that he had to forget feeling and look emphatically to the future. For the future was by definition a place without feelings as well as, in his view, a place of greater measure and science, in which individuals would be submitted to a grand collective effort.

His foul mood that day resulted—nothing could be plainer—

I.I. Magdalen

from having been forcibly tugged back into the past by some officious, moralistic American and by Nous Taad's muffled warnings.

While shaving in the icy water, he thought of Taad's telephone call as if someone from the distant past—perhaps his father—were reminding him of some ancient peccadillo. Something annoying, but in no way arousing his conscience.

He recalled perfectly how he had felt when the businessman called. At most, it would have been to invite him for a quick drink to discuss union affairs at the Bauwerk or to make sure that the party in Brussels felt the same way as the party in Liège (which Tamas controlled). There'd be a little head-knocking, some sharp bargaining. But nothing personal. They'd been allies long ago, and Nous' first money (big money, not the sort of small change everyone made on the black market during the war) had become Kekes' first campaign money. But no one had ever intimated they were friends. They weren't. Tamas had no friends and Nous had too many of the wrong sort.

Then Nous mentioned Emma and the American. Tamas thought Taad had to be joking. Why would anyone be asking about Emma H. any more than anyone ever asked about Jeanne?

But Nous hadn't been joking. His tone was as matter-of-fact as if he were cutting a deal with the city fathers for a new stadium for Standard, the town's football club, or housing for immigrants (safely tucked far away from the battered old center). This man he hardly knew and hadn't seen for over three decades, apart from the occasional business meeting or in union negotiations, said, He's asking questions, that's all I know. I said I'd see him. It's safer that way. I'll be able to find out what he's really up to. I'll let you know. Don't call up, don't come by.

He had sensed in Nous Taad's voice his deep distaste at having to talk to him at all. He wouldn't have told that snotty secretary he slept with to get Kekes Tamas on the line. Most certainly not! A set of circumstances had brought the men together. Briefly. That was what happened in wartime. And after that they had had little to say to one another. Nothing personal.

But the moment Taad had called, paralysis had set in. Five

days had gone by and still Tamas had no clear idea what he was going to do about that otherwise neatly excised moment in the past. Or what he could do. He hadn't thought about Emma H. in years, nor had anyone else.

It wouldn't be true to say he'd forgotten Emma. She was not that easily erased. To the degree that he'd seen her physically at all clearly (before the end)—and he hadn't felt it quite right to look at her directly when she first walked into union headquarters to volunteer—he knew that this was no Jeanne. She was terrifyingly different. Not sick; radiant. Not clinging; firm, upright. Not wily, not smarmy. Direct.

He'd mumbled something about being grateful for any help they could get and why, er, someone in her position…

What position is that?

…I mean, well, you seem…

I am rich. That's not seeming is it?

I meant, your reason. And he couldn't get out more than that.

And she'd laughed.

I need a reason to help?

Well yes, he thought. I don't know you from Adam. I do know you as Eve. He said, This is a place for working people. I shouldn't have to explain this to you.

I think that if I need a reason to help I don't want to help.

Then Tamas thought, who sent this girl here? But he saw no way to find out without engaging her in further conversation. And that way lay danger.

That had been in the winter of 1941–2.

Yet when he met her again, she—a mere schoolgirl—had written him an enormous check, and on a hard currency bank, in favor of the Lowlands-Soviet Friendship Society. Again, he hadn't really dared look up at her properly, but he sensed that she was smiling again. She said, If you're me, you help who you want. Isn't that what you do?

Of course it had gone on from there. He had taken what she

said to be mocking him, accusing him of insincerity, even hypocrisy. He had tried to explain—there had been plenty of occasions and he couldn't ever be certain who actually made those 'occasions' possible: had he? Had she?—but they all sounded far too personal. And when he did feel that he was expressing his convictions in a purposeful way, he saw that she was totally uninterested in politics of any kind. Hadn't she said as much? That she was curious about what people were, not what they did? And how would one know what they were, really were, unless it was in some relationship far more passionate (that was the word she used, and he misread) than politics could ever provide? Politics, she said, was about the future. Then she'd come up quite close to his thick glasses so that he could see (greatly enlarged) her great, green eyes and said, Where does that leave *now*?

What was *now* was that every morning he woke up thinking the American would find him and want to talk. And he hadn't, which made him both grateful and increasingly nervous.

But Sunday struck him—Sundays always struck him—as an ominous day. Just the sort of day an American would call.

He could tell his landlady, who was Indian and fat on the proceeds of a half-dozen laundromats she and her sons controlled, not to take any calls. But what if it were one of the other boarders who picked up the phone in that obscenely over-decorated parlor full of bejeweled elephants and other gods?

Then he thought that if he weren't at home, no one could call him. The first step, then, was to dress and get out of the house.

When he'd done so and gone downstairs, he wrote his name and the hour in the little book by the telephone and called Felix to cancel the usual Sunday morning study-group (scheduled subject, Pierre Naville and the Trotskyites) because Taad and Bernard both knew his habits and they might find him in the rear of the billiard-hall where the local party held its meetings.

Or run the group yourself, he said to Felix, giving him a brief and hurried outline of the talk he had sketched out.

When he got out into the street, he was quickly soaked

Emma H.

through—buses didn't run very often on Sunday, least of all in this remote part of town—and the only thing he could think of was that he should see Bernard. Even though Bernard would have no desire to see him.

Chapter seven

Private lives flow backwards. Or they did for him, Henning thought. You met someone, perhaps you'd been told something about him beforehand, then after a lunch or a dinner or a quick drink, you thought such-and-such about him. You met him again and he might acquire a past, or he'd be with a woman you didn't know he was with. Bit by bit, there were revelations of a sort. Desirable or undesirable. And almost always going backwards in time.

Sometimes you never got to know very much. No matter how hard you tried to find out.

Non, mon cher Commissaire, he said to Masquelier—even as Kekes Tamas was walking from his prole *quartier* towards the *Centre Ville*—one doesn't often get the truth straight. And no question about the past is entirely innocent (He thought, Oh, your father killed himself? Gosh. Why?) so no answer was unvarnished.

The *Commissaire* wasn't often to be seen in town on a Sunday. He was an enthusiastic fisherman, an avocation so foreign to his looks, his profession and his general comportment that it surprised even himself to have such a passion for it.

Emma H.

But perhaps for this American, he could use fishing as a sort of metaphor. There were dark waters, there was bait, beyond the bait was a hook, at the end one might (or might not) land one's fish. But he wasn't fishing, he had sent out for coffee and he and M. Forsell were sharing it on a nasty rainy morning. To his surprise, he liked the young man. Half his age, but polite in the way few young men were after '68, when the young began to think they'd unlocked the secrets of the universe and that the freshness of their experience (whatever it was, sex or drugs or crazy paintings) was infinitely superior to his forty years of experience with human beings of every kind. So instead of metaphors, he expressed his views on Bernard Pons. As simply as he could.

That wasn't entirely easy. He had little time for intellectuals and even less for Bernard Pons.

The man looks like he was born in a cassock, he said. One would think he'd spent a lifetime confessing elderly ladies. Ladies who by definition had no sins except the ordinary ones Pons himself had—avarice, gluttony, nostalgia, and the fear of death. You'll get nothing from him about Emma H. Pons is discretion itself.

You've known him a long time?

I've lived a long life doing dirty work. He poured a little cognac from a flask into his coffee and added, One gets to know a great number of people. Yes, I've known Bernard since the war, when I came back—unbelievably young, fresh and proud of myself—from the Congo as a Detective Sergeant. He too was a fresh graduate—from Louvain, he had thought of being a priest—and had just begun to work in the city archives. Police and Archives go together. You are right to esteem, and fear, the past. Mark though, I didn't say Bernard wouldn't know about Emma. She was not an unknown person here, even when very young. What I said was that he might not tell you much.

Henning sensed that Masquelier's own reticence was not unlike Bernard's or Nous Taad's or for that matter *Mevrouw* Kerkevelde's. What he did feel (because he trusted the *Commissaire*) was that if Masquelier were hiding anything from him, it would be for a good reason, so he didn't put any more difficult questions to him.

There would be a reason why he wouldn't tell me much?
Isn't there always?
The trial, Henning said. You would have known about that?
I knew about it after it was over.
From Bernard Pons?
And from others.
May I ask you what you know?
Masquelier relaxed. As to the trial, he was on safe ground. What happened afterwards was not safe ground.
He explained.

It wasn't a proper trial such as the official trials that were held in the immediate aftermath of Liberation in 1944. Tamas Kekes was secretary of the communist party, with connections abroad that made life for him during the occupation exceedingly difficult. He was never in one place for long and at some point much of his partisan network was rounded up. The logical supposition was that they'd been betrayed. By whom, nobody knows. Maybe not even Kekes. He certainly convinced himself that Emma did it. That she had somehow had access to their code-names, *a* code-name even, a planned meeting. Whatever, Kekes was not around when the Gestapo fell on them. Which is why not a few people think that Kekes himself may have eliminated his own people: as rivals, as not toeing the right line, as knowing things about his own activities they ought not to.

That's your view?
It is probably Bernard's view.
And it was not a fair trial.
No. Emma H. is the name she was given by the British authorities. She was not on the Belgian wanted list. Her aunt was, but not Emma. Most people thought she must be dead, somewhere in Russia.

But the trial wasn't stopped. I mean, the government didn't intervene? Seek to try her itself?
It was very quick.
There were no questions afterwards?
Everyone had questions. But there were no answers.

Masquelier suddenly felt weary. He too had hoped not to be dragged back into that particularly unpleasant part of his own past. But his guest showed no signs of impatience and he obviously could not be turned away. Not considering the influence he had in Brussels. Not taking into account that his own retirement was due to take place in a little over six months. Just stay away from the part when Kekes' van appeared and took off to Nous Taad's lodge, he thought.

So he said, Emma H. had been held at Roetgen on the German border. She had simply walked right through the frontier station without looking left or right and as though she'd been marching like that—which is probably not very far from the truth—for thousands of miles. She was stopped. Not because she didn't have the right papers, but because she had no papers at all.

All right, so she is brought to Headquarters for questioning. Plenty of people in her situation. Germany was still a mess. Belgium was coming back to normal. But Emma is not 'many people'. Emma is Emma. Not much of her is left. But some things are. She is a young woman. She may be hollow-eyed and a mess, but she gives off a certain authority. And she speaks perfect English to the corporal who stops her.

However, she also refuses to give her name or where she is from.

She says, I am going home.

It is a young British lieutenant who questions her. He has missed the real war. He has only just been called up. He sees her standing opposite his desk in semi-military tatters like many German civilians in the last weeks of the war. She looks desperately thin and perhaps mentally disturbed. He asks her her name. She says, Emma.

He says, Emma what?

She says, I don't know any more.

She could be telling the truth, she could be lying. At best she is another Displaced Person. One who speaks excellent English.

He asks where she has just come from.

Berlin.
And before that?
Perhaps Russia?
She puts a question mark at the end of Russia. As if she really didn't know.
He says, Would you like a cup of tea?
She nods and smiles, and when it is brought she cradles it with both hands like something infinitely precious.
He sends for bread-and-butter. The poor girl is starved. Nonetheless, she eats the bread with great delicacy. But she is also distracted. The lieutenant is sorry for her. He thinks she may be one of the stragglers who escaped Bergen-Belsen when it was freed. Someone might have looked after her and she was only now making her way 'home'.
He asked her if she was Jewish.
She said, No, I am a Catholic.
Where were you going? Which way?
She wipes hair away from her forehead. (Oh yes, it is all very clear in Masquelier's mind! Every image. Every word. He interviewed the young lieutenant and he hasn't forgotten a word or a picture.) She says, I think I have family in Eupen, but she can't remember a name. She thinks she remembers a house in the forest. In a clearing.
Remember, his job is not easy. He has only a half-dozen men under his command and his orders are to make certain the border remained closely guarded, even in small villages like Roetgen. Refugees from France and the Lowlands are fleeing westward, Displaced Persons slip out of the camps that had been set up for them. German deserters or escaped prisoners, various Cossacks and members of Vlasov's army, collaborators are all working their way eastward. The war is over, but not the general catastrophe, not the settling of accounts.
He has a social instinct, this lieutenant. In his eyes, this is not just some ordinary D.P. If he acts on his own authority—his inclination is to let her through—the result could be tricky. A girl like that, who knew who she knew?

He has a way out. Her real identity is not settled. He sends a message to British Army headquarters in Hanover and meanwhile forwards her to Aachen, 'pending identification'.

What do you think, M. Forsell?

The trial stinks, that's what I think. In the papers you kindly gave me—most useful history—I gather that most of the 'collaboration' had already been accounted for. Twelve thousand names on the official list, a few hundred executed, a few thousand serving time in prison, and a fair number 'missing'.

Like Emma.

She must have been mad to try to come back.

Or she had received assurances.

Not from her aunt. Her aunt was off on a cruise.

There are other possibilities.

Henning nodded. Yes, too many. She told the young subaltern she was going home. To what?

Chapter eight

Pons was extremely regular in his habits. Every day except Wednesday, when officially he took the train to Mechelen to see a mysterious 'sister' of his, he could be found at the same table in the Liegois, an old-fashioned brasserie around the corner from the City Hall.

In his own way, Pons had become untouchable. When Henning had called asking to see him, he asked no questions at all of Henning—not who he was, what he wanted, how Henning knew his name. Masquelier's image of the priest in his confessional was exact—people came to Pons, he didn't go to them. He was an archive himself, he expected to be consulted. He simply said that he always ate in the same restaurant at the same hour and was not averse to company.

The Hoofrads? Yes. I knew them well. I was the girl's godfather.

You couldn't be much more explicit than that. Unless one added—as Bernard had—that the girl was called Emma because her mother had been a devoted reader of English novels. And to that,

that her whole family were Protestants, but she had chosen to be a Catholic.

A demain, then? He said. See you tomorrow.

A man sure of his ground.

Henning got to the brasserie a few minutes after noon and with a waiter's help found Pons in the far back of the murky room. He sat with his back to the room, as though he didn't want to see anyone.

What sort of a man sat, always, in that curious a place, Henning wondered. A secretive one? One who didn't want to be seen, or one who didn't want to see?

Then he saw that it was not entirely so. There was a mirror (engraved 'Stella Artois') on the wall facing Pons, as though deliberately placed there, a mirror in which Pons could watch. Which was not, of course, the same as seeing.

Certainly a man of habits.

Then a curious thing happened as Henning worked his way down the center aisle towards Bernard's table. In one moment Henning could see a huge soup-spoon halfway to Bernard's mouth, had time to note Pons' thin lips, his cropped hair, an expression of remoteness in his eyes, and in the next Pons had stood up, and walked towards the door. Startled, Henning stuck out his hand. Pons walked right past him.

When he turned around, he saw Pons talking gravely to a thin gingery man with meager sandy hair and beer-bottle glasses, a cloth cap in his hands, thick heavy boots, and a denim shirt.

Whatever the two men had to say to each other was quickly over, but the overall impression it made on Henning was distasteful. The man with the cap obviously had something urgent to say and had come some ways to say it (he was thoroughly soaked). He expected to find Pons there as usual. Yet Pons didn't want to listen to him at all.

A brief, nasty expression of class?

Then Pons came back down the aisle of the brasserie, and, barely stopping, said *Venez*. Meaning come. Do what I say.

Henning took the seat opposite Pons, and quite as though

nothing had happened and without a word, Pons continued to finish his soup, blowing on each mouthful as though it were too hot. Which it couldn't be.

Was this staged for his benefit? As an expression of imperturbability?

Henning tried to imagine Pons at more or less thirty, the age he would have been at the end of the war. A few years out of the seminary. He concluded Pons had always had the same table. And a breviary in his pocket?

Pons had already ordered for them both. The waitress brought a rich carbonnade and then, shortly after, one of those splendid burgundies in which Belgium specializes.

So now, Pons said, how may I be of assistance to you?

Delicious, answered Henning, who was seldom disconcerted. You are a gourmet as well?

As well?

As well as being a man of archives. (And quite possibly one of those paradoxical ascetic gluttons.) Emma is my *sujet du jour*.

Pons was amused. You are writing an essay?

That is more or less what I do.

Then don't include that little scene at the door. That was one of the Unholy Trinity that so interests you, Tamas Kekes.

I'd guessed as much.

He sees plots everywhere. Whereas I find your curiosity quite natural.

I shan't write about the scene at the door. But I do expect to see M. Kekes.

Good luck. His usual tendency is to vanish. Into the Caves of the Kremlin. Tell me, whose version of Emma is it you would like?

Yours.

Bernard looked offended by the bluntness of the answer. He was used to greater subtlety. This didn't bother Henning, however. At the moment he was casting his line into a dark, empty sea and he was expecting little or nothing from Pons—that is, beyond the obvious question which he could neither ask nor expect to have answered—why, if Bernard had been a friend of the family and the girl's godfather, had he taken part in ordering and carrying out Emma's execution?

Having allowed some time and many mouthfuls to go by, Bernard finally said, Could we start somewhere else? For me, you see, she is a difficult subject.

Why was that? Her death was difficult, she was difficult, their relations were difficult?

You're thinking there is some deep, dark secret between us. There wasn't. (Though there might have been, Bernard thought. And of the four men who'd been closest to her—Kloosters, with whom she went off to war, Father Krzysztof her confessor, Andrzej and himself—who knew the most secret parts of her life best?) That is, no more than there was a secret, dark, dirty or whatever, between Emma and everyone.

Pons repeated it: *everyone*. Everyone who met her, spoke to her or knew her at all.

Then where would *you* like to start? Henning said.

You no doubt started with some image of her…?

You mean a photograph? Henning nodded. Her aunt sent me one.

A religious image!

Beautiful.

Young, vulnerable, lofty, reserved, fetching! The sacred image of *la jeune fille bien élevée*.

Which meant, Henning knew, a great deal more than a 'well-brought-up young lady'. It implied standing, correctness, self-discipline—the accumulated arts of the upper classes.

And she wasn't?

She was a saint, Bernard said, finishing his wine. A saint and a devil. Look at what she did to the people around her, to satisfy her own fantasies! (If the American only knew about those letters of hers, thought Pons. Desperate and trivial letters, a jumble of girlish fantasies and womanly despair. Letters from which one could really

I.I. Magdalen

learn nothing. How could Henning understand that, he who had never held Emma in his arms?)

What Bernard Pons had most dreaded was happening and—intelligent as he was—he felt incapable of doing anything to stop it.

First there had been hearing she was alive (a word from Conincq, her old notary), then her abrupt arrival on the spot—on her way, away, anywhere! Then that stupid trial, the ride in the cold and the rain up to Nous' lodge with that fool Kekes, the arrival of the others, the denouement. A period of banking up the fires, the return of her aunt, the by-play of the pianist on one side and of Taad and Kekes on the other—that had taken a year or two. Then had come the long silence, which had lasted years and years.

Then Tante Berthe, hurtling into her stolid eighties, had suddenly thirsted—for the truth? Or for the money?—had taken it into her head to publish that fool letter in the local papers. As though she didn't know what would fall onto her head!

A year later he was facing this young man. Who would gnaw at the bone.

It was a process he detested. In his world, acts were acts. He could live with acts. One can live with sin. Sins and acts were recorded and were parts of larger events. He could be forgiven (so could *she*) but there was no going back on what had been done…

Forgiven but not forgotten.

In his experience the one thing that could not be reduced to an archive—to classification, a dossier, a file, a sheaf of papers, these being the proper end for the contentious, let future generations judge of motive and context—was sin. Sin continued to live within one until one died.

And sin was something, Pons thought, that he and Emma shared. Not that they had sinned together, but that they had each, equally and separately, sinned. Those separate sins were what had brought them together on a given day.

That being so, Pons could hardly help himself. With this uncomprehending man facing him, sin too had to be explained. It had to be put into context and motivation, to be translated into personality, character, opportunity, shading.

And where did that start? Why, with Emma herself, obviously. He heard himself saying to the American, The little bitch (he meant the expression to be affectionate) *lived* for us, we were part of what she wanted.

Who was this 'us'? Did this Forsell know about the others? All the others? He'd been to see Nous, but Nous would have said nothing interesting, he had nothing interesting to say. Ever. Bernard had forestalled Tamas at the door. No doubt the American would find him. But then Tamas had very different things to say to him; and much more on his conscience.

Anyway, what he'd just said to the young man wasn't entirely true. Emma hadn't so much lived for them as died for them, which was a completely different matter.

It was all right for Nous to say—he was always a bit player, always on the fringes, half-gardener, half-poacher—that the American was not an official, not a policeman, not an arm of any tribunal. He wasn't. It didn't follow that 'He can't do us any harm if we stick together'. He was Berthe Kerkevelde's 'representative'. At the very least, he was armed with a moral right to know.

So there were some things one could say to the man, and others that one couldn't. One could, for instance, tell him that Emma had always been hunted. And hunted herself. She still appeared to him regularly. Unchanging. The way he'd first seen her as an odd child, then as a young girl with healthy (and unhealthy) appetites.

There was that candor, those innocent light-green eyes. Eyes like a spring meadow. How could anyone resist? She was neither woman nor girl. She was all the bits and bobs men ever wanted, and her body was more than a man could safely dream of.

Himself excepted of course, because it hadn't been her body he craved, but her dangerous soul!

Ridiculous even to think of saying to this young man that he hadn't fallen in love with Emma at the font, but not long after—when still a child, solemn, alone, sitting at the piano—sometimes with the old family notary, Conincq, seated and listening alongside him, rapt, his eyes glistening.

Kekes. The Pole. Kloosters. God only at the end.

Pons woke from his reverie and mastered himself. He knew he had to warn the American against the scrawny, servile Tamas. He said, Kekes was Confidant and Commissar to Emma. Emma always *supported* the weak. But she only *loved* the strong.

That was the man you went up to when I was coming in? Why did you send him away?

Because the very sight of him made Bernard sick, though that wasn't what Bernard said.

Bernard had done his duty. He'd warned both Emma and her Tante Berthe about Tamas. He'd said there were midges and motes and mitochondria as small as Tamas and as meddling. Beware of them! His apparent frailty is the source of his power: and his desire to destroy you and your kind.

All he said was, Kekes is an interested party and therefore not to be trusted.

Is it that you simply dislike the man? Henning asked. Or is this a political statement about Kekes?

Bernard bought some time: You mean, do I like this or that man? Then the answer is yes. I dislike him greatly. Politically—I suppose you mean that he is a communist, a Stalinist—I'd rather stay ambiguous.

Only when they parted did it occur to Bernard that the American had looked at the photograph and he'd fallen in love with Emma—as so many others had. He probably didn't even know that he had.

Not very far away, trudging towards his union hall through the rain, Kekes Tamas fed on even richer resentments.

First he imagined Bernard at table. Offal would be piled high before him. Lamb kidneys baked in their fat, thick slabs of calves' liver drowned in caramelized onions. He didn't envy Pons the food, only his relish for it. He felt nauseous.

At the local café where he and the comrades met or ate, he

stopped, because he was hungry and wanted to dry off. He had a coffee and a slab of bread and butter. He read the party paper and a two-day-old *l'Humanité* from Paris, bought his daily *Milde Sorte*, smoked one or two and then hesitated. Had it been really wise to walk in on Bernard like that? Even to let him know that he was worried?

That bloody old fascist aunt of Emma's had written something or other about it in the newspaper and impugned (though without mentioning names) the 'revolutionary justice' meted out in the aftermath of the war. And should she complain? She should have been shot, too. As he'd said to Nous at the time, What's that stupid fat woman complaining about? She had collaborated as much as her niece—though not as dangerously—and nothing had happened to her. So why was she quacking now?

He lit another cigarette.

Nous had said he would be back in touch. He hadn't called. Yet he had met this American.

Tamas certainly wouldn't put it past Taad to blab the whole story to the American and blame him, Tamas, for the incident. After all, he had fired first. And they'd both—Nous and Bernard—equivocated at the trial. Which was why he'd included them among the execution squad.

He was solid, Bernard and Nous were flaky. He was the real thing, a professional and a dedicated revolutionary like his father before him.

The bar was comfortable. He was known there, he felt safe there (the owner was a member of his executive) and he could think there.

He looked out through the fogged up windows and saw it was still raining.

It made him angry that this free time, rare enough in his life, should be taken up by a woman long dead.

Comrade Lenin thought speculation and doubt were the fatal defects of intellectuals. A real revolutionary set a plan and carried it out ruthlessly.

That had been the case in 1945. The girl had been taken out

to Nous Taad's hunting cabin and shot. The three of them had fired together. He had held the flashlight and pointed it at her. She had looked him right in the eye and he hadn't felt a thing. Why should it be different now?

As so often in these circumstances, Kekes thought back to his own youth, to what his father had taught him about Bela Kun's glorious revolution in 1919–1920, the very first after the USSR's! Back then, there'd been no sentimentality about enemies of the people, no more than there had been over the Tsar's family. Back then, the spoiled brats of Budapest, those Hungarian Emmas, had been turfed out of their jobs and estates; they'd been reduced to two shirts, one suit, one pair of shoes, and made to share toilet facilities with real worker families.

Tamas would have killed the lot. Then there'd have been no Admiral Horthy to clap his father in jail for ten years and make a boy like himself live like a mole, hunted from place to place and job to job. Luckily, some of his father's party friends had got him out in 1938, first to democratic (ha!) Czechoslovakia and the following year, via Spain, to France. Where he received new orders.

That train of thought brought him back to the urgent meeting over which he (appointed by the Central Committee of the PCB) had presided. At the very tail end of the summer of 1945.

No, he didn't want to go back there.

Then, suddenly, he saw her again as he'd seen her with his own eyes. On parade! With the fascists! The pious, hypocritical little bitch! By 1943, she was off with the volunteer SS legion to fight in Russia. Against Bolshevik Power! She had risen like a V-2 rocket.

They wanted more to condemn her?

He heard again the scraping of wooden chairs on the tiled floor of the billiard-hall where the trial had been held. He could smell the beer and the perfumed tobacco that had just come back into the shops. He remembered pulling at the moustache he had then (not unlike Comrade Stalin's) to conceal his impatience with those who said they hadn't survived the war to start killing young girls for some foolishness. At least the few his wretched eyesight let him see.

Foolishness was it? He'd had to put it to the executive committee straight, in a manly fashion, before they moved on to the membership waiting in the union hall.

Let me remind you…

It hadn't been a 'scientific' decision. Feelings entered into everything. They were sick of the war, they were already beginning to forget. Their bellies, their hearts, their sorrows urged clemency.

He remembered standing up before them and imagining himself standing over Emma and cutting her throat if that was what had to be. For the party, to be sure, but also for his wife, for Jeanne. Yes, Emma was lovely. That was another reason for despoiling and humiliating her, for disarranging all that beauty.

Chapter nine

It was still drizzling on Monday morning. At about eleven, Mlle. Pascal stood at the window of her office. Uppermost in her mind, which brooded endlessly on her marital prospects (she was thirty-seven and there wasn't that much time left if she wanted a family of her own), was where her boss could be going so early for lunch when there was nothing of the sort inscribed in her agenda. Thus she saw the whole thing.

It was indeed, as she—a student of the cinema—said, surreal. *Comme du* Buñuel. One moment Nous was striding out the front door towards the company parking lot which was across the street, as always, in a hurry; in the next frame a cyclist, in no hurry at all, was coming down the street towards him; and still later, the camera a bit out of focus and without sound (she never heard the shots—there were four of them—through the plate-glass), Nous fell to the shiny cobblestones, the cyclist continued by, and…well, it was so much like a film, so surreal, you understand, at first she didn't believe the evidence of her own eyes.

The whole thing was impossible. Utterly impossible.

Mechanically, she called the police—that too was part of every film—and in a daze, not daring to go down and tend to the man she loved and from whom she got so little in return, she awaited their arrival. She spent the time, until she heard the police alarms, rifling through his desk. In part in search of that Other Woman she was convinced existed and in part for papers Nous might not have wanted the police to see. She was nothing if not efficient and in less than two minutes the desk Henning had seen in chaotic disorder was clean, and—Mlle. Pascal reflected ruefully—as trouble-free as though the man had never existed.

When the police did arrive she was already protected by the icy calm of one who knows nothing but does her job (organizing someone else's life) with impartial, scrupulous care and loyalty. In five minutes, she had created a script in her head and settled, like a veteran of film noir, into adopting a supporting role.

The office, *his* office, had become a set. The rain beyond the window was artificial. The director, megaphone in hand, was consulting the script-girl and reminding her that in the previous shoot the secretary's hair (her hair) had been worn differently. Which she diligently restored to the way it had been when she stood at the window.

After that the lines had all been written for her. She described the scene over and over again, practically without a change in her wording, letter-perfect except for matters of interpretation of her part, now distraught, now grieved, now outraged.

Nous striding, as though in a hurry (she explained that he was always that way, so active and *sportif* a man) across the street to the company parking lot and his Mercedes; the way, from a corner of her eye, she had seen a lone cyclist coming down the street (not very busy in what was still mid-morning); and then the way the rider of that bike had reached into the little basket in front of his handlebars—Yes, it was a woman's bike, perhaps stolen?—and, reaching Taad, had aimed directly at his chest as Nous turned around. Possibly in answer to a call. That was a conjecture, she said, since she could hear nothing. As in a silent film. And continued on his way.

No, no hurry, no change of pace, with perfect *calme*. She was sure it was a man. Not a very big man. No, not a young man either, she thought. Someone perfectly *ordinaire*. You know, the kind of person you see every day. Like Dan Duryea, the actor?

He wore a beret and he cycled with his knees out, the way people do who are not so often on a bicycle. No, she could not be more specific.

Did she have any idea who might have done it? None. Did her employer have any enemies, personal or otherwise?

There she parted with her script to say tartly, Of course. Everyone has enemies. Except the insignificant.

She bit her lip and said more modestly, Particularly a man of M. Taad's prominence.

He was going out. You know what he was doing? Who he was seeing?

He had no lunch scheduled. She looked at her wristwatch (a present from Nous) as though he were still alive and she had to remind him of an appointment he had.

You will forgive me for asking—the inspector sent along was young, and blushed—but were your relations with M. Taad entirely professional?

This question (the answer long readied in her mind) she handled *de haut en bas*. M. Taad, she said, was a gentleman and a professional. He did not mix business and pleasure. Nor do I.

When the police had gone, it was time for lunch. At the restaurant where she usually went, there would be people asking questions, so she walked in the opposite direction and stopped in a wine bar, which had just opened. *Bon Dieu*, she thought, two changes in one day! And laughed at herself.

Then she returned to the office and behaved as she did every other day of her life. She was used to dealing with the most intricate parts of Nous' enterprises. These must not be allowed to falter. Whoever took over the company would need her.

At six o'clock, as on every other day, she locked up Nous Taad's office and then her own (which adjoined). Monday evenings she had her hair done. It was half-price night.

To lie back in the huge chair, her damp hair wrapped in a cloth, was very relaxing. The results seen in the bank of mirrors before her were comforting and remote. At most, one might detect a slight thickening of her neck or, closer up, a delta of tiny tracks at the corners of her eyes.

While she leaned back, she thought things through. What would happen next?

The police would be a nuisance, but no more than that. What had happened was so senseless, so directionless and arbitrary that if it made no sense to her who knew more about Nous and his affairs than anyone in the world, it wouldn't make much sense to the police either. They would take it for granted that she was Nous' mistress. In fact, they probably knew that already. And if they knew that, they knew that she not only had no reason to kill him but every reason not to.

Then would come the lawyers. She had already contacted Coquin and indicated her availability to help in any capacity while refraining from asking any questions about the murder—lest she be told something she did not want to hear or be thought to be asking indiscreet questions about M. Taad's will. Coquin had seemed pleased with her co-operation.

During the week, she supposed the Bauwerk board would have to meet. The financial condition of the company was not at its best and Taad, who held a forty-nine percent interest, had been drawing against his shares to finance his campaign. No doubt a way would be found.

At that point she lost track of Nous' doings for a while, as her hair was being combed out and arranged.

I am not going out tonight, Willem, she said.

Then I shall leave you as you are.

She took that somewhat gloomily, as a sort of epitaph.

It was then that she thought about the rest of Nous Taad's life.

I.I. Magdalen

About all those parts of it to which she was not admitted, in which she was left exactly as she was.

Opportunity presented itself. She had her own keys to Nous' apartment. She would not be able to keep them for long. Nor would she have any reason to use them. If the police had come at all, they would also have gone. The concierge of the building knew her and knew she regularly visited. If anyone asked, she had but to say that she had left some papers behind and had come to fetch them.

She also knew—as she knew the combination to the safe in his bedroom (You know how I am, he'd said. I'm likely to forget the combination!)—that his important private papers were kept at home.

She got to Nous' apartment on foot in less than five minutes. Of course the silly concierge, a Mme. Poniatowska, stopped her by the stairs.

What a dreadful story! You must be terribly upset. Can I get you a cup of tea? Or perhaps a drink?

I have things to do upstairs. All files have to be returned to the office. I hope the police haven't made too much of a mess.

They were very quick.

She was a greedy little creature, Mme. Poniatowska. Will you be on television tonight?

Me? Mlle. Pascal laughed.

They took pictures of the building.

The moment she started up the stairs, she had an uneasy feeling. She couldn't have described exactly what she felt. Only that she who had been so sensible, so in control of herself all day, was somehow—imperceptibly—no longer *in charge*.

The apartment was only a single flight up, but on every step she seemed to get a new instruction—now there was too great a slit in her skirt, now her brassiere was disengaged, her heels made too much noise, her stockings weren't on straight. As though someone were criticizing her.

At the door, it was that her handbag was a mess and she couldn't find the apartment keys quickly enough, that the light was on the left—no, on the right.

Only the thought of all the things she'd done for Nous over the years steadied her. He'd be grateful to her for going through the apartment and making sure everything was all right.

Would there be money in the safe? (There usually was.) She wouldn't touch it.

Her hand was on the light switch. Should she turn it on? Supposing the police had left someone behind to keep a watch? She knew murderers often returned after their crimes.

She decided she wouldn't take the risk. She would pull the curtains if they weren't shut and just turn on a single light in the bathroom. Yet even as she felt her way down the hall—making sure she *knew* what she was doing, that someone else wasn't guiding her steps—she felt a horrible compulsion to see the apartment one last time. Their bed, the fireplace, the carpet by the fireplace, the master bathroom where she did her douche afterwards, the one drawer in the spare-room cupboard where she kept a few necessities, her sanitary napkins, a spare nightdress.

The thought of what she had lost—hair done for nothing, for no one, a solitary supper at home, spinsterhood, the children that should have been hers—suddenly hit her with force, such that she had to go through to the drawing room and sit down.

The crime was senseless, heartless. Worse, she knew that in the milieux that Nous frequented—building materials, trucking, politics, property—few would mourn him; only a woman such as herself could be truly attached.

Which reminded her that she ought to (Why now? she asked herself) see if there were any traces of other women in Nous' apartment. She despised herself for this stupid jealousy, but she could not help herself.

First, however, she rose from the sofa and went over to the bookcase. The little safe was behind several bound volumes of sporting and motor racing magazines on the shelves to the left of the fireplace. One pushed a button and a section of the bookcase sprang open.

Deftly, she dialed the combination and pulled the door open.

Inside were three or four thick envelopes, a leather bag, a small revolver, and a bundle of documents, which she recognized as deeds on property Nous had recently acquired near the airport. The leather bag she knew. It contained sentimental trinkets—a brooch that had belonged to his mother, his Resistance medal, his scout-knife from childhood. Under the revolver was a bundle of bank notes in denominations of one hundred thousand francs.

None of that was compromising, so she took out only the revolver and the envelopes.

As she did so, there was a sudden chill in the room, as though a door or a window had just opened and instinctively she put the envelopes down and shut the safe door before turning around. It was just an illusion. She was overwrought and perhaps because she was she could not rid herself of the feeling that she was being conducted through a series of movements—to come from the hairdresser here, to find the concierge with her door open, to take the stairs rather than the elevator, right down to the order of the rooms she'd gone through and even the sequence of her thoughts.

The weight of this subservience was not unlike her feeling toward Nous Taad. It was oppressive because its limit was unknown, because she had served without term or promise or contract. She had done everything for him in the office and then—whenever asked—whatever he wanted in bed.

It felt just the same as that just at that moment. Her eyes were heavy, her legs tired, her pelvis was bearing her down as darkly as gravity—as when Nous used to beckon her into the bedroom. Wordlessly. With just his index finger. And shut the door behind them.

She knew she was going back there. She would be fine if she lay down. She would take her clothes off and get between the sheets. Then she would have a short sweet sleep and things would be as they had always been.

She took the gun with her, but as she left the room, she threw the envelopes onto a nearby windowsill, where they remained hidden when she drew the curtains.

These two little acts of independence—taking the gun and hiding the envelopes—were probably what saved her.

When she came back out into the hall—one had to get around a monstrosity she'd always hated, a little china oriental gentleman who held a light concealed in his turban that never worked, and it took care—she found herself confronted by a man, and he, expecting that he was stealing up on her, found himself confronted by a woman holding a revolver in her hand which was pointed straight at him.

Neither of them saw the other clearly, Kekes because of his eyesight and she because she had practically run right into him and had a gun in her hand as well as her heart in her mouth.

The difference between them (and Kekes had to make an instant calculation) was that she did not know who he was, whereas he knew who she was and had reckoned she would come back—like a loyal evening ghost—to clear up Nous' many messes.

Take the gun from her and she could identify him. Kill her and he was asking for trouble.

He chose the easy way. He charged at her, hit her as hard as he could, pushed her to the ground, ripped open her dress, and pulling it up over her head (she didn't scream), ran into the drawing room. His good ears had heard the tumblers fall when she opened the safe, had seen (through a mirror that stood opposite) where the safe was, and had not heard the firm clicks he would have heard if she'd shut the safe properly.

He helped himself to the money and the leather bag (she was a thief or she had interrupted a thief, let her tell whatever story she wanted) and ran out of the apartment, leaving open the kitchen door leading to the back stairs through which he had come in, and down to the bottom of the stairs and out. Stopping, until he was sure the concierge was back in her apartment.

If he hadn't got what he wanted (those papers that Nous had

always threatened him with), nor had she. It was also perfectly possible that there *were* no such incriminating papers.

His comrades would see to it that he'd never been there. He hadn't been there at all the entire day. He'd been in Mechelen.

His luck remained poor and the money would be a consolation.

Chapter ten

Henning was heading towards Maastricht when he heard the news on the radio. The radio treated the murder—and the evening television and the next day's papers took the same line—as connected to politics or business. The coverage struck Henning as subdued, even mechanical, and lacking the key ingredients of Sex and Money. As to the politics, Nous had been planning to run as an independent (the media only grumbled and wondered who would gain from his death). As a businessman, only his money was respected. His war record was mentioned and a late story just before Henning went to bed said that his apartment and safe had been broken into. As for the man, it soon enough seemed that he'd never been there.

The Dutch papers in Maastricht editorialized that Nous Taad hadn't been a bad man but he hadn't been a good man either. Was he on the take? Quite probably. Ordinary people don't get tempted; it's hardly worth the effort. But politicians do it out of habit; it's a perk of the job.

All of which was deeply irrelevant. Henning knew why he'd been killed. Because he was no longer a young man, nor even a brave man, and he got careless. Henning didn't know why, but he was quite certain he'd been killed because of Emma.

Once questions began to be asked, all three men directly concerned in her death should have been worried. Quite simply, they all hated one another. And perhaps now also hated what had happened long ago. If Nous knew something the others didn't, then it was logical that he should have known he was a target. Why didn't he do anything about it?

For the three days he spent in Maastricht, as Taad's death faded gently from public view, the murder remained unexpected and unsettling for Henning.

That is, he had half come to the conclusion that all three members of the shooting party had long ago agreed on a story and shared the burden of sticking to it. Now that was up in the air. Someone didn't agree. By nature Henning disliked coincidence.

From his picturesque hotel—all gables and lace curtains—he called Masquelier.

He said, Shouldn't we at least keep quiet about any connections to Emma? Let the public assume—as it seems to—that if there's more to Taad's killing than meets the eye, it must be Money or Sex? What about Taad's secretary?

She got a nasty beating.

The jealous mistress?

Both jealous and his mistress. She says she went to his apartment to pick up things that belonged to her. She says her attacker must have taken the money from the safe. What I didn't like was that she didn't call us.

She didn't see her attacker?

We had bad luck on that score.

And what do you mean, she didn't call you?

Just what I said. When she came to, she called a taxi and took herself to Emergency. Arrived half-undressed, with a shopping-bag, and said she'd been attacked on her way back from the market. They fixed her up on the spot and sent her home. We got the report Tuesday morning. *Bien sur*, her market story didn't hold up. But she wasn't keen to talk. Anyway, she's not central to the story. She's just an accident along the way.

Pons? Kekes?

Bernard is certain it was Kekes. Kekes hasn't been seen in Liège since you and Bernard saw him on Sunday.

Henning said, He was after something. Was Taad blackmailing him over something we don't know about?

By the laws of logic, it should be he who would be blackmailing Taad.

A man like Kekes wouldn't kill unless he panicked over something.

It won't be over your girl. What's the worst that could happen to any of them if the trial and execution weren't entirely kosher? A reprimand? The state's not going to open up the case after all these years. And not *just* because your Emma led an unappetizing life and met an unappetizing death. There wouldn't be any point.

I agree, said Henning. There's something else. And that something else is connected to back then.

The 'back then' was where Henning was. He walked about Maastricht as though buildings could talk, and parks, places where she might have lived or played. One of its high solid houses could have belonged to Emma's family. This was where she had been orphaned. It was here that someone must have come to the house to give her the news. And it was here too—at the age of ten—that she'd had to absorb the fact. Whether or not she was close to her parents.

The town and its unanswerable questions tired him. As usual, looking into the lives of others invariably brought him back to himself, of whom he always asked the fiercest questions.

Often this happened by exactly the sort of ridiculous coincidence that he so despised—as when leafing through the necrologies in the *Limburgsch Dagblad* he came across the deaths of Emma's parents.

She was an only child and her father Willem had been a professor of Roman-Dutch law at Leuven, while her mother, Isbel Kerkevelde had been a painter (he went to look, after lunch, in the local museum) of traditional, cool, precisely-lit still lives. They were good paintings, and no doubt Willem had been a fine jurist.

Nonetheless, a certain sadness clung to all three of them: not just the sadness of being cut off in their prime, but the stillness, the fixity of their lives. The absence of any real connection among the three of them: as with dead parents to whom reference is never made.

This obliqueness was further emphasized by the mystery that clung to their deaths, for no cause for the accident that killed the parents seemed to have been established; no more than with Emma's death. According to the paper, their car, a Mercedes, had been examined without result. The day had been sunny, the traffic light, the road unencumbered. And yet to all appearances, Professor Doctor Willem Hoofrad had driven straight into a tree on an August afternoon in 1935.

Their deaths had occurred (hence the long delay in reporting them) on the very same day as another tragedy, the death of Belgium's lovely and beloved Queen Astrid, in Küssnacht, Switzerland. August 29th 1935. Coinciding with a royal death, their deaths, and the pain of the loss, had been diminished by the coincidence, to relative unimportance, though it cannot have been unimportant for Emma, who shortly thereafter had to be taken into her Tante Berthe's house.

That the Queen, who had been at the wheel of her car, had died because she was seized by a sneezing fit brought the matter close to Henning, whose father Bjørn had several times told him the story, calling the Swedish Queen's death a 'stupid death'.

Henning's father's death—he was a man who had given much thought to death—had been no less terrible for his son, but had been calm, untroubled, and intelligently conceived; Henning wondered if that was not also true of Willem Hoofrad, and possibly, too, of the lovely girl known as Emma H.

There were people who courted death, and he seemed surrounded with them.

Chapter eleven

With the American sitting opposite him—very firm, very sober, and probably right, though he wasn't ready, just yet, to admit this—*Commissaire* Masquelier spoke more shrilly than he perhaps intended or should. That was because he, too, felt weighed down by this old affair, to which he knew, but the American so far did not, he had certain 'connections'. He felt his thin hair was stragglier than ever. His seat, as he sank down into a chair that had never been comfortable and was now even less so, had expanded. But not his brain.

There were some things he had to say, others that he wanted to say. However, it was in his nature and in the nature of his *job* to allow others to speculate freely, to come up with all sorts of fancy theories while he—trying hard to appear imperturbable—had to deal with whatever random facts appeared to fit the case he was working on.

That was why his men had been out and about in town taking pictures of men who in some way resembled the killer Mlle. Pascal had seen from Nous' office window. Men in raincoats, men wearing berets, men on bikes, men of a certain age and as *ordinary* as he could find. About a dozen of these had been collected and Masquelier—seemingly on a whim of his own—had added four men to them, two of whose pictures required 'doctoring' by police artists to conform to requirements. So far as Masquelier knew, two of these were 'known' to Henning: Kekes and Pons.

A fairly recent picture of Kekes leaving his union hall after a meeting had been given a beret the Hungarian (who strongly favored caps) had never worn. Pons was another difficulty since he never exercised or used a bicycle. He did wear a beret and a raincoat.

The other two men were people the *Commissaire* knew had connections to Emma but Forsell presumably did not. Masquelier was wrong about the first (Andrzej Niemczyk) but that was because Forsell—he said chidingly—had not been forthcoming. He was right about the second, Father Krzysztof. Both men had been photographed on bikes and wearing berets. Mlle. Nicole had hardly hesitated. She had put a delicate finger on the snapshot (somewhat out of focus) of the Polish pianist.

For Masquelier it was a useful identification. It gave him time. It satisfied his bosses in Brussels who were always itchy about politics.

Furthermore, there was the question of his dignity. It was one thing for the young American to call him up and advise him how to run his shop, it was quite another to tell him to his face that not only was the old Pole the wrong man to arrest for the murder of Nous Taad but that he proposed to do something about it—in fact already had done something about it, depositing 500,000 francs (no inconsiderable sum) with his new friend Jacques Coquin.

The *Commissaire* knew Coquin well. As he explained to Henning—trying to show friendliness—Coquin was a man of sudden fortune. Both money and luck had played a big part in his life. Not old money but perhaps old luck. But Coquin was not the man he would have entrusted with a delicate case.

Maybe so, said Forsell. But all the man's got to do is find a decent lawyer. Every man needs a friend. I can't see that Andrzej has any others. And M. Coquin is available. Willing. Concerned. He does represent my client's interests. That is, Berthe Kerkevelde's interests.

I.I. Magdalen

The *Commissaire* nodded sagely. To him, Coquin's interests and Berthe's interests seemed much of a muchness. In principle, Coquin might well be the man to find M. Forsell—if money were no concern—the very best lawyer in Wallonia. But down in the gray world where he lived, Masquelier thought the American was taking a big risk.

Coquin had begun by handling Berthe Kerkevelde's interests—that is, making sure she was safe from disagreeable consequences for her wartime entrepreneurship. But ten years later, when *Mevrouw* Kerkevelde bought him the Conincq *cabinet*, matters were less clear.

Masquelier had understood early in his long career that human greed was among the most powerful of motives. He thought Emma's Tante Berthe and Jacques Coquin had more than their fair share.

And in this instance, the American was putting a spoke in several wheels. Masquelier felt his standing in the city and his rank in the police were being challenged by a *bien pensant*, a do-gooder, who had no idea the sort of cowpat he was stepping in. Did the man think he was an utter fool? After forty-one years of service (minus the war)? Of course the killing of Taad had its political fall-out, and he was inclined to think perhaps also a political motive. One doesn't shoot prominent citizens and potential deputies just for fun. On the street? In the fresh air?

By the by, he thought, just where had Nous Taad been going that morning? *Who* did he have such an important and urgent meeting with?

That was a subject on which Mlle. Pascal had been un-illuminating. Though she too was greedy. And now deprived.

No, no, he thought. This was altogether an unfortunate *conjoncture*, an unhappy meeting of minds on the wrong side of the political fence, with which he, *Commissaire* Masquelier, had to deal. Every policeman, however high his rank (or perhaps the higher the more so), swims in a political sea.

Consider the presence in Liège of M. Forsell. How had he come to be here? Just now? Through Berthe Kerkevelde, definitely a figure in conservative circles and certainly no friend to the likes of Nous Taad.

And how had Mme. Kerkevelde found this blondish American with so many languages, a personal fortune, and the silly ideals for which his countrymen were known—not to speak of a very fetching and young wife (whose picture was in the middle drawer of his desk, face down)?

That hadn't taken long to find out. Through Notaire Coquin, inquiries had been made at a certain private bank in Brussels with extensive holdings in Central Africa (formerly Belgian, the *Commissaire* thought regretfully, who had begun his career there) and the politics to match.

Unfortunate, no? That the bank had picked on *him*, on this particular young man? Why had the old woman and this Levantine *creep* suddenly re-opened an affair so long dead?

Cherchez l'argent, he thought. There had to be money at the bottom of it. Whose money? Well obviously Emma Hoofrad's money. They wanted to know what had happened to it. At the very least that was Coquin's motive. Who knew where it was, eh? That was something he would rather only a very few people (himself among them) knew. Because if that was found out, all the rest would come out, too. And better, all around, that it shouldn't.

But one had to face the facts. There M. Forsell was. Sitting opposite him and quite rightly pointing out the sheer flimsiness of the case he, *Commissaire* Masquelier, could make out against a poor, old, incompetent Pole.

But the Pole, *merde*, at least existed. He was to hand. He was helping to keep the whole affair of Nous Taad's death quiet.

To gain some time and marshal his arguments—arguments he felt he *had* to make—he buzzed for his secretary and asked her for coffee. Did M. Forsell take sugar? He did. Good. An excellent idea. Coffee without sugar was an abomination, and bad for the stomach.

About the bicycle, Henning said.

I.I. Magdalen

The bicycle was found at his house, Masquelier said, his voice rising in spite of himself.

Which bicycle?

The bicycle the man used when Taad was shot.

Describe it.

A woman's bicycle, old, dirty…

Found at his house?

Yes, leaning against the back side.

But I was there a week ago. There was a bicycle there, his bicycle. Also old, also rusty, also dirty. Only it was a man's bicycle.

Masquelier didn't exactly gasp. He ruminated, he belched into his hand. This was disconcerting and far too close for comfort. He was slipping up. He had become complacent in his old age. The American had found the Pole? How? Masquelier grinned thinly, keeping his patience for the moment. Why didn't the woman bring the coffee, so that the American would stop telling him what he already knew? And so he could make this new fact fit in with the rest. *Merde*! Once you get a Polish drunk talking, he never stops.

He struggled to gain time and composure. He said, There was no man's bicycle there when we went. Just a woman's bike like the one Mlle. Pascal described. And the tire marks? M. Forsell? You recall it was raining. We photographed them at the time. We cannot be absolutely sure until we get a report back from Brussels, but they would seem to be very much alike.

How many thousands of bicycles have the same treads, *M. le Commissaire*?

With the same patterns of wear?

Probably hundreds, if not thousands. Not stuff that would stand up in court. What a bluff! Americans surely didn't ride bikes.

Anyone could have brought the bicycle to his house.

And the weapon? What about that? Neatly wrapped in a plastic shopping bag.

No fingerprints of course.

Masquelier kept a straight face. He said, No, it had been carefully wiped.

Then the same argument prevails: whoever brought the bag brought the gun too.

It's an old gun, a Werther. From wartime. A German officer's gun.

Fortunately, the coffee arrived, and Masquelier had a moment in which he could mutter to himself that if the shoe were on the other foot, he would be arguing as Henning was. And to consider why he was so unreasonably irritated with what was taking place on his patch.

Answer: He anticipated nothing but trouble from the muddy waters being stirred.

The case had nearly cost him his job when he was a fresh-faced junior inspector 're-integrated' (that was what they called it) from the colonies. He remembered the very senior *Intendant* who asked him point-blank, *Quoi au juste faisiez-vous dans cette galère?* Just what in hell do you think you are doing messing about in this business?

Well, back then he'd known just about as little about Emma as M. Forsell knew about her now. He had acted according to his own intuition of what was right and wrong—because the people who had urged him to act were at the very least the *kinds* of people he thought the police should be backing. Only later had the less savory side of the lovely, exhausted Mlle. Hoofrad surfaced. In the debris.

He, too, had not known much about the past. Ambitious young men—and he had been one—were not attracted to the complexities of history. Oh no! And to boot, he'd been off among the *nègres* in the sweaty tropics. He knew next to nothing about Rexists, communists, the 'massacre' at Courcelles—only that the brother of that Liège notable, M. Georges Simenon (his very favorite writer!), had been involved.

M. Forsell was working (as he had been) with received opinion. With the story Berthe Kerkevelde had chosen to tell after nearly four decades of silence.

Her story fitted. More or less. There had been hasty decisions taken in the aftermath of war and occupation. They weren't all just or wise, but they had been taken and that was that. There was no going back on them. But Berthe's story was only one way to look at Emma.

He wanted to pat the young man on the hand—as older, wiser men do with the innocent and the young when they are about to lose their illusions—and say, Silence is golden. Loose talk is dangerous.

Merde again. In what way was he harming that poor, wretched Pole, who at least would have a week or ten days of square meals and a warm bed? All he was asking for was time. But every time he looked into the American's deceptively innocent eyes, he felt the man knew that and wanted the same thing—if for a different reason. That was why he was pressing so hard. Too hard. He had an agenda. Everyone did.

Masquelier felt he was a reasonable man. If the American could read into his old cop's soul, he would see that someone like himself couldn't possibly approve of someone like Nous Taad. The man had sticky fingers. He was greedy.

By arresting the Pole he had produced a 'result'. It wasn't one that would stand up. Bah, to hell with idealists!

Mlle. Nicole identified him.

Forsell said, That's all?

What more do you want?

I want it to make sense.

What makes you think it doesn't? At least for now?

Because I've met the man.

And you don't think he was just crazy enough to do something like this?

Obvious suspects are so convenient.

Now you're going too far, protested Masquelier.

Sorry.

I have worse for you. You know what our Niemczyk lives on?

Church money.

And Nous Taad.

What?

Masquelier grinned thinly. He said nothing immediately but handed the American a thick sheaf of papers.

Monsieur Taad's bank accounts. Check the totals underlined. They amount to a fair sum of money, by the standards of a poor man, anyway.

The American registered neither surprise nor dismay. He simply asked, And you conclude?

I would have thought blackmail was an obvious possibility.

Niemczyk kills the goose that lays the golden eggs? What does the man himself say about those payments?

Nothing.

He does not deny them?

He neither denies nor admits. I'm not sure he's aware of what's going on.

Why couldn't the young man understand—without forcing him to say so—that he'd arrested the Pole strictly *for his own protection*?

Because he thought 'Police'. He and Forsell started at opposite ends. A policeman—to a young man without direct experience of police work—is a man who's grown up in a certain culture. In a dense world of like-minded men bent on solutions. To Forsell he presumably was an abstraction. Policing was an administrative task. There was public order to be maintained.

What a luxury to be a *philosophe* and dabble in human stories!

Can I see him? Henning asked.

No. At least not right away.

Chapter twelve

Kekes Tamas was in yet another bare room when he learned from a comrade in Liège that a Pole had been arrested for the murder of Nous Taad. He knew the Pole as he knew his bare room. The only thing one brought with one to such places and such people was history.

The arrest pleased him—it was all in all a surprising bit of unexpected justice—and so did the room. A room in Mechelen not unlike this one was where he'd started his life of exile, where Jeanne and he had lived and where she'd died.

If you looked back at your life, the party, his party (that curious word derived from taking sides), was the only kind of family he had, or wanted. Not the child Jeanne hadn't had. Not Jeanne herself. Because the party—even as it paid for her funeral and his comrades brought flowers—transcended mere circumstances. So long as one was faithful, it took care of its own.

Similarly, the enemy would always betray himself—as had happened when Emma came back from Russia. She went right back to the snug bolt holes she'd used before. She wanted to flee to Spain with her lover, Kloosters. It was the Pole she went to. The Pole would set things in motion for her.

The important thing was to have been *right*. Right about Emma, right about Nous, right about history. Right about women and feelings.

The American was thirty-something. According to Nous, he had a pretty young wife. She had to be a distraction. He had no distractions.

It was harder to stick to the true path at sixty than it had been at twenty. There were compensations. He felt he had Experience. The young American didn't. He was naked as a kid playing on the beach was, innocent of history. Hiding in his bare room in Mechelen—surrounded by newspapers and provisioned by good, reliable friends—he felt the strength of his long struggle. His history had been *lived*. He had learned how history *imposes* itself. Yes, sometimes it was regrettable—in human terms. Many of the men the Germans had taken away were his old friends. But they'd read their history wrong.

Henning's problem may not have been so different.

Everybody here told him that he couldn't possibly understand what it had been like—during the war, after the war—because he hadn't lived through it. But of course that was foolish. You didn't need to die to understand something about death. That was why human beings had imagination.

What people really meant when they said that was that he wasn't *them*, that he didn't live in their skins—so how could he know what it was like for them?

By the same argument, he wasn't a woman—much less a beautiful woman—so how could he understand Emma?

The hardest thing of all to understand was her appalling indifference. Her failure to resist when it finally mattered terribly, when it was a matter of her life.

She was *perfect*, Ludi said one night. And perfection was a terrible burden. It set you apart from ordinary human beings. She giggled. Like being a virgin.

In the early morning, the *Commissaire* called up. He said the Pole had signed a full confession.

Chapter thirteen

There she was all right. An ordinary station, a grainy cigarette-littered platform, a gray train, and unsmiling men leaning their arms on its lowered windows. On the platform—recognizably the same girl despite the banal wartime two-piece, grown-up suit, straight-skirted, and a little pillbox on her head that covered that high brow—Emma.

Next to her—her arm slipped through his sleeve—was a man in uniform. Among a half-dozen others, though the only one actually touching her. They were looking straight at the camera, pleased with themselves. The men in the train behind them looked down toward them without visible feeling of any sort. The photo was dated 1941. Emma was fifteen or sixteen, depending on the time of year.

This shift—from girl in the earlier photographs to woman in this one—was disconcerting. It was as though they were two different people. Something had been lost of the girl. Had something been gained by the woman? When Henning held one photograph up next to the other, the physical changes were easy to discern—a richer flesh, more rounded, a different glow, something infinitely less lofty and almost domestic.

Finally, it was the men on the train who retained his attention. As members of the Flemish Legion off to fight the Bolsheviks, they should have been smiling, waving, smoking, bearing flowers. Their cause was triumphant. But they didn't smile. Emma did. And so did—looking down into her face—young Kloosters.

The way she clung to that uniformed arm, and the fox at her neck, indicated submission. It was a uniformed arm—with its own barely discernible device on the shoulder, something to do with a cross. Emma had embraced a certain kind of politics, and too, precociously, a man (an officer) perhaps twice her age. The get-up, gloves and hat and fur at the neck, said 'mistress'. No innocence there. Two young people with assumptions about the future—that it was going to be good to them. But they also saw themselves as outlaws, gallant, quixotic figures.

This was the picture (bannered throughout the press) that had so infuriated Kekes Tamas. She was a turncoat.

Henning could feel the shock himself. He felt that he had been betrayed. On what basis did one turn against one's neighbors and friends? What did it mean? It meant that something others cared very deeply about was of no value at all to the betrayer. It was like that in life and marriage; it was like that in war. Betrayal always hurt more because it was intended to hurt more.

Also, because she was a woman and everyone who knew her had wanted to love her.

He was unable to sleep. After several hours of wrestling with his duvet he got up and went to the window. It gave out onto a narrow side street.

A couple was walking up the street. Well apart. The woman was ten yards in front of the man (her husband?) and arrived first at the door of what appeared to be their modest house. She went in and turned on the light. Henning thought the man would just follow her in. He didn't. Instead, he squatted on the stoop as if he were sulking or trying to come to terms with some terrible piece of news.

I.I. Magdalen

He stayed there a good fifteen minutes. Then the woman turned off the light in the house and at last he went in.

It was wretched and drizzly, a typically rotten, Belgian, May night. What was going on? He felt he had seen—at a great distance—some private tragedy. The tragedy simply emphasized that all round him there were secret lives. About which one could know nothing. In the same way that Emma must have come back from school one day to hear that her parents had been killed. From which moment she had become a different girl. One marked by fate?

He felt he had to see *Mevrouw* Kerkevelde, who had said nothing at all about this man—with whom Emma must have spent the last four years of her life. He needed to know more, much more, before passing such quick judgment on Emma.

So in the morning, he went back to Liège and called Coquin. His clerk said the notary was not available.

Given the mood he was in, he was furious. He said, I must see *Mevrouw* Kerkevelde. I will be at his office at six. Then he hung up.

In Henning's world, the law had always been important. In Oklahoma, it seemed one of the more solid edifices. Who had helped the ten-year-old Emma?

There was a man always called 'old M. Conincq.' He too would have to be seen. He lived over in Tongeren. He must have been for Emma what Mr. Henry Hatfield had been for the young Henning. Mr. Hatfield—complete with his powerfully stained pre-war fedora—had been a powerful presence back then. Henning recalled the hours he spent in Mr. Hatfield's Tulsa office having explained to him with patient sympathy just what the Forsell oil-leases amounted to.

He was no Coquin. Nor was Judge Wittig, who had rocked, wilting, on the hot Forsell porch and discussed such vital matters as taxation law in regard to undeveloped property, unexploited oil leases and the niceties of offshore banking. No Coquin indeed. These and others were men of a certain hard probity, plain men with old-fashioned desks and courtliness, with squeaky wooden chairs and ticking clocks. They had done what they could—for his father's sake—to mitigate the fall-out from his rash, solipsistic suicide. Henning was grateful to them. As a man climbing a steep cliff is grateful for a firm foothold.

There didn't seem to be many such here.

The reassuring seriousness of equity was not what one first thought of when received by M. Coquin.

Instead of a cramped office with books to the ceiling, and dockets, depositions, and files tied with blue ribbon, he found himself sitting in a spacious room in an old and high-ceilinged private house. There M. Coquin presided behind a Louis XIV desk, greatly decorated with gold, while Henning was offered one of several tufted leather chairs, all silky soft.

It was more boudoir than office, but Henning was not deterred. The time had come to draw the line on the kind of well-heeled seduction, the silky silence, in which money did its work.

It is something one can't take with one, Henning said. One's money. I suppose the question is, where is it? What's left of her niece otherwise? There should be papers, letters, school reports, medical reports, baby pictures, ledgers, Monsieur. With Emma, everything is missing. I do not believe your client knows nothing about this deposit, about what survives us. I insist on seeing her or I will simply abandon a task that I was led into—and these are her words—by curiosity.

No, no, Coquin said in his oily voice, my client was very explicit on this point. She didn't want to influence you one way or another. It's for you to find your own way.

I can do that, Henning answered. But what if your client does not like the result?

And anyway, Coquin purred, what if it all turns out to be no more than a wild goose chase? I advised her strongly not to pursue the matter. What good can come of it? The 'truth' is not always helpful.

You talked of 'discretion'. There is a difference between discretion and concealment.

She is a lady of a certain social and financial standing. You have to understand that these are delicate and perhaps even painful matters for my client.

Excuse me, said Henning, trying hard to control himself. They may be delicate and painful to her. They were *fatal* to her niece. And now they seem to have become fatal to another of your clients, M. Taad. You don't seem much distressed. Yet the police are bound to ask awkward questions.

Apart from at last getting to see Berthe Kerkevelde, the rest of the meeting was just as fruitless.

Turn over a rock and you're likely to find a rattlesnake.

Chapter fourteen

A 'companion', sallow and slender, the color of blotting paper (her name was Bintje), brought Henning upstairs to the informal drawing-room where Berthe Kerkevelde spent most of her days. With the TV on. If Bintje was slender as the old Dutch house in Mechelen (and like the house of a wilted red tulip color) where she and her employer lived, Berthe was heavy and solid as old furniture. She had cropped white hair that curled closely and copper-colored freckles, big hands (they trembled) and ankle boots.

A plain woman, it was her way to deal with the world as it was, with herself as she was. What she thought, she said straight out. Without preamble, she handed Henning a newspaper clipping. She said, Sit down and read it.

He did.

Sirs,

In the late summer of 1945, my niece, known as Emma H. in the reports you published at the time, was summarily 'executed' without trial by a group calling themselves members of the maquis. Many

Emma H.

terrible things were done during the war and should not be forgotten. Other terrible things were done at the Liberation, and they should not be forgotten either. No charges of active collaboration were ever entered against my niece and no evidence exists of such collaboration. I hope it is never too late to enquire into the exact circumstances of my niece's death. The persons who committed this act of revenge are still alive. She was, of course, not the only victim of the settling of accounts that took place in the last months of the war and in the year following, but she is the only one whose judicial murder, so late in the day, has been left un-examined by the Authorities and forgotten by the community.

Yours, etc.,

Berthe Kerkevelde.

She said, Officially nothing happened. No one paid any attention. But of course the communists and the rest of those '*resistants*' fell on me like a ton of bricks. It was like water seeping under the door. Rising all the time. I tell you, there was some very private hatred involved. It's unpleasant to think that someone hates you enough to threaten you, to destroy you, perhaps to kill you. Especially at my age. I am not blameless in life, but I didn't think I deserved that kind of hatred. When they wouldn't go away I sought some help. *Private* help. I wasn't going to get any anywhere else.

You waited a very long time, Henning said.

I know, I know. It's hard to say this to someone, but Emma was on my conscience. I'm afraid this is all going to sound very terrible to you. It is perhaps why I wanted you to work by yourself—knowing that in the end you'd find out about me. How does one say this to a foreigner who is young enough to be my grandson?

There's no humiliation in the truth.

There isn't, M. Forsell? Now there you surprise me. You don't feel any better by knowing the truth about yourself. You feel far, far worse. You are deserted by all your illusions. The truth about me is that I couldn't face what I'd done or rather what I'd failed to do. It went on for years, eating me up. I *hated* the girl, I *wanted* her dead.

Nee, nee, Bintje said. You must not do this to yourself.

With every word Berthe said, the tall old upright house grew more lugubrious. Dark concealed portraits on the walls, carpets sank into their tiled floors. Old histories lapped at the foundations of the house, of this solid old woman, at her fortune, at the life that was ebbing out of her.

Henning let her talk. She was old, she was lonely, she was afraid. There was also a concentration of bitterness and envy in her. What she needed was to tell someone. At last. Now he saw what his intended role was. Perhaps always would be. To hear the self-accusations of the desperate. Which bring no comfort at all.

Somehow a bottle of Alt Genever appeared on a tray. Bintje hovered anxiously, then sat on a low stool by Berthe's solid legs.

There had been three of them in the family, plus Emma of course, and now they were all dead. Her older brother Pim ('I worshipped him when I was young') had been killed in the last days of the war. The Big War in '14–'18. Her clever, beautiful sister Isbel was killed in 1935.

She said, If you want to think of fate you could do worse than start with my name, Berthe. What does that name bring to your mind? A Berthe is a big, horsy woman. The others were elves, fairy creatures. When Pim died, my father put me right into the business. I started at sixteen as his secretary. Invoices, accounting, bills of lading—Berthe will do it! Someone had to make sure of the beautiful and talented Isbel's future. Being a painter is more valuable than being a bookkeeper. He counted on me. Or he took me for granted. You're the *reliable* one, he said! And I was. I became, and always have been, the family workhorse. I wasn't suited to anything else. And when my father died in the influenza epidemic after the war, I took over from him; to work and get rich was my destiny. Forget about men, love, children, art, elegance—all that belonged to *them*. Did I get any thanks?

She watched them from a distance. They had all fallen to her. All the tedious realities.

I became, she said, like a good Flemish house, transparent. We don't shut our curtains. All those interiors you've seen in paintings are there to tell you that the people inside lead clear, clean, irreproachable lives. Let them look in and see how much money you have! Money becomes what counts. My life has not been irreproachable, but what you see is what you get. A life of money.

You ask yourself, but Berthe, who are you doing it all for?

For that perfect couple, Isbel and Willem? A romantic death on the same day as our Queen! How well stage-managed! While I struggle to keep our businesses going among a sea of unemployed. And their beautiful, artistic, talented daughter falls to my lot. She put me in my place quickly enough!

I stood in the cemetery on a horrid hot morning. The place smelled of rot. You wear black like a nun and it sticks to your body. The girl stands some way off chewing on a blade of grass! She has no more connection to her parents than I do. I see she couldn't care less. M. Conincq—who is to look after her unearned fortune—is the one with his arm draped over her shoulder. The place is full of officials, the *Burgemeister*, the curator of the museum, old men in tall hats from the university. It's very solemn. She looks down at her feet and I am shocked. She is wearing a pair of patent-leather pumps. Dancing shoes. Does she mean something by that or is it another sign of her inability to step outside herself? How would I know?

She sees me off at the station. The windows of the train are wide open with the heat. She reaches up and extends her hand—in a white glove, like a little princess!—and says, I hear I am to come and live with you.

I look in vain for some idea of what this means to her. So far as I can see it means nothing at all. Was she like that with her mother and father?

She had no idea of their relations, as family. Once a year for a week Emma would be sent to Berthe's summer home in Zandvoort. She'd come and she'd go and you'd not know she'd ever been there. She embroidered, she played solitaire.

When I was out of the house, she played on my piano. When I came back, she stopped. As though her music didn't belong to me.

Bintje said, You mustn't tire yourself *Mevrouw*.

I'm not tired. I'm sick at heart. Look at us. Look at how bored we are. Bored with life, bored with each other. Once a week we have company, don't we, Bintje?

Oh yes.

My doctor, my notary. People from a former life. We eat and drink too much, we play bridge.

And when she came to stay? said Henning.

To stay? She was out the door like a shot. It's a terrible thing to say, but we didn't *like* one another. I don't mean that she was a bad girl or that we had arguments and she was rude. Nothing like that. I'd rather we had argued.

Bintje said, What *Mevrouw* means is that the girl was proud. Too proud for ordinary daily life.

That's not quite it either, Berthe said. It was in her bearing. The way she stood. As though one wasn't allowed to touch her. Yes, the way she stood before you. Feet slightly turned out like a dancer. Defying you to find anything wrong. And there wasn't anything wrong. She was obedient—even humble about some things. Clean, neat, first in her class, always on time.

Berthe leaned forward and put a hand on Henning's knee. She said, One wanted to take a chocolate pudding and drop it in her lap!

Berthe's laugh was coarse. And filled with long-suppressed rage.

And there was religion, Bintje said.

And there was religion, Berthe picked up. She wouldn't go to school here. I was informed of Mademoiselle's desires by M. Conincq. He said to me one day, She has made arrangements to board with the sisters in Liège. Just like that.

Bintje clucked, I don't know how she did it.

Of course, she had her own money. She could afford it.

She would never have lied. That was not her style. She would have said she was going to Liège and simply gone to the school. The nuns would have taken her in.

Imagine, Berthe said. Not a Catholic in the family for I don't know how long—four hundred years? She did the same thing with her mother. Didn't tell her. Simply went to a priest and said she wanted instruction. Went to a family friend in Liège and asked him to be her godfather. They never said no to her. They didn't *dare*. No one said no.

That's M. Pons.

Yes. She made a funny sort of life for herself in Liège. The nuns didn't say no either. She came and went pretty much as she wanted. Somewhere, there are stacks of correspondence with the good sisters. They don't dare say she's 'uncontrollable'. They just can't control her. Like every girl her age, I suppose she had some favorite nun who made her escapades possible. By 'escapades' I don't mean anything shocking. The rest of the girls were locked up at night. Nine o'clock, lights out. That's how it was before the war. But she? If she wanted to go to a concert, how could they refuse her?

The music, said Bintje. You must tell your guest about the music.

I have no ear for music but what I heard from the school and the Mother Superior was that she was very 'gifted'—whatever that means.

There was a compromise in the end, you remember? You told me about it. Her godfather was allowed to take her out.

A man of irreproachable conduct, Berthe said with brutal sarcasm. He showed that in 1945!

How much was she here? Henning asked.

Here? In this house? Hardly at all. I put my foot down with M. Conincq about the holidays. I said a girl of twelve—however advanced—is not mistress of her own destiny. Whatever she thought. She made no difficulty about that. 'Of course, Tante Berthe.' I got girls to come to the house. They had parties, outings, my chauffeur drove them around. They were all terrified. She was at another level of existence. She'd read books they'd not heard of, she didn't plod through a version of *für Elise*, she dressed simply, but in things from the very best shops, from Brussels or Paris (things her Godfather or

M. Conincq bought for her)—No wonder they all fell away! As you say, she was exceptionally beautiful. But apparently quite untouchable. Boys were out of the question.

Why? Little girls dream of boys.

Little girls? Don't mistake the Mona Lisa smile or that mysterious look. She was *never* a little girl. Not her, Berthe said sternly. The 1930s were a grubby period. Dirty, dark, despairing. She was attracted to that. I heard once from Pons who was called up right away. He said something like, We've lost her.

I lost touch with her the summer the war started. I heard she'd left school and thrown herself into music. That summer I wrote her, I tried to find her in Liège. It wasn't until September that I got a letter from her. She said she was fine and that I needn't worry about her. It was a very impersonal letter and at the same time very *aware*. It was the same old story. She had no needs. Needs were something other people had. She said that everyone had something missing and she would try to make up for it. To fill the needs of others. At the time, I wouldn't have been surprised if she had an adolescent fixation with Jesus or Mary. You know, devote herself to God the way children often do around death.

But that wasn't it at all. I got her to agree to see me and in September I met her in Liège. We met in a café. She looked more beautiful than ever and I thought, she's in love, she's become a woman. This is while she's finishing off the last of her ice cream. Delicately, the way she did everything.

Was there a man? I asked. She looked at me completely without expression. As though anyone could see men were out of the question. She said she was a musician and would never marry.

Why not? I asked.

She said very casually, I expect to die young doing something exceptional. Something exceptional and *anonymous*.

That was the last time I saw her.

Henning felt a chill. He thought: To die young and anonymous. What could that possibly mean?

Mevrouw Kerkevelde, solid as she was, looked tired. She said, I see you wonder the same things as I've wondered all these years. What did she mean by that? Did she think of it as a fate or as a choice?

A silence settled in the room. Bintje fidgeted on her chair, upright and thoughtful of the old lady's moods.

Finally Henning said, Maybe the important thing was not to be what she had been—the *jeune fille bien élevée*. As for anonymity, what could be more anonymous than not to have been buried, or for no one to know where she lay?

That hurt as much as the guilt, Berthe said. I couldn't bear the thought of her lying there in the ground like that, the life gone out of her. After what she went through in Russia and Berlin at the end. It's *wrong*. I'm glad you found her Polish friend. I…Well, I didn't know which side he was on…

Just then the phone rang and Bintje went into a neighboring room to answer it, while she and Henning sat in silence.

It's the police calling for you from Liège, she said when she came back.

He picked up the receiver in the next room.

M. Forsell? Masquelier here. Niemczyk is in the Police Hospital.

He's ill?

He tried to hang himself.

Chapter fifteen

Hanged! The words, the act, its images, scurried through Henning's mind like anxious rats in a maze. He drove back to Liège seeing against the lights of oncoming cars broken necks and bodies swaying in the dark. His father blurted onto his windscreen like a bug, asphyxiated.

Why did hanging carry greater opprobrium than leaping out of the forty-first floor or shoving a shotgun in one's mouth? The exhibitionism of the act? The absurdity of the spectacle—the reduction of the human body to useless laundry swaying on a line? No, it was that he could take death in most forms, but not the way which made it so hard to forgive his father.

At the hospital, he found the *Commissaire* by the Pole's bedside and a *gendarme* stationed at the door.

Almost, Masquelier said. Very close. A few minutes more and he would have succeeded. Incompetents in the cells, Monsieur. I regret that this happened.

Henning looked down at the man in the bed. Andrzej looked much reduced in size. He was curled up into a tiny ball of striped, unbuttoned pajamas like someone from the camps, ribcage exposed and heartbeat jumpy, a thick dog-collar of bruises on his neck.

What happened?

At least you and I don't have to ask why, answered Masquelier. Not yet. What happened? Simple. Early morning. No one paying attention due to the change of shifts at six. He took off his belt, knotted it round his neck, tied one end to a hook on the back of the door and slumped down to the floor. Only the buckle on his belt was worn and broke loose after a while. He'd tried again with what remained of the belt but couldn't tie it properly. Finally he tore his shirt into strips, wetting the strips and winding them into rope, and tried again. This time he was nearly successful in choking himself: until breakfast time when a nurse tried to open the door and dropped her tray. She cut him down.

Another debut performance, Henning thought. Another failure. Who will hand Andrzej the flowers this time? Still, he was sore with the *Commissaire*. It had been a crackpot idea to arrest Niemczyk and have him confess to the thousand guilts that preyed on his weak mind.

He said, Now what? You don't think you were playing with a man's life?

Masquelier looked like he could use a drink.

Niemczyk was bait, he nodded. To that extent, yes. I would love it if life gave me an exquisite balance so that I didn't have to set a goat out to catch a wolf. You think I have time enough to weigh one nicety against another? Of course Niemczyk didn't kill Taad. Kekes did. But your Pole is hiding things too.

For hiding you can't do much better than being dead.

Masquelier gave an expressive sigh and Henning felt a moment of sympathy for the *Commissaire*. After all, Masquelier hadn't asked to be dropped into this mess.

He said, chiding, You knew where I was in Mechelen. You've had me followed?

For your own sake. We think that's where Kekes is. You could have been in danger. Kekes' motives for killing Taad have to be powerful. In 1945, you could get rid of your enemies with some ease. This isn't wartime any more, so he has to feel remarkably sure that he can get away with it. Otherwise, he wouldn't have gone back to Taad's house.

He was looking for something.

Something Nous maybe kept in his safe. Certainly not for the money. People like Kekes despise money. Mind you, I wouldn't be surprised if Mlle. Pascale didn't take the money herself. She could have felt it belonged to her by right. For years of faithful service.

Emma's aunt wasn't specific, but she says she was threatened. I would guess also by Kekes.

Almost certainly by Kekes. His unions control her factories. It's been a Thirty Years War between them.

And Emma is a part of that war?

Could be. She complained to us several times in the past year. There was nothing we could do. They were anonymous letters she got. Kekes is no fool. No, I think the person who has most to worry is Mlle. Pascale. No, no, don't worry. We have her under surveillance. If there was something in that safe, it's a reasonable presumption it's in her hands. If it was something on Kekes—and he and Taad have always kept up relations, not cordial relations but relations—then she'll want to use it against him.

You think she knows it was Kekes who attacked her?

I'm pretty sure. One has to remember Mlle. Pascale has a rich fantasy life. She went to Taad's place to help him out, probably. But also for a chance to imagine what it might have been like to live there with her boss. To lie in that bed and think of it as *hers*.

Andrzej stirred.

Poor son-of-a-bitch, Henning said. Nothing ever went right for him.

I think he was terrified.

Of what?

Of being forced to say things he knew.

Henning thought back to his meeting with Andrzej. The feeling he had that the Pole had already pulled the plug on his life. Perhaps

Emma H.

until he had arrived on the scene and started asking questions, Andrzej had simply forgotten that he intended to kill himself.

Henning came back several times over the next few days. Andrzej healed slowly, but also cunningly. Sometimes he thought the Pole was playing at being senile. Or was it that his mind just came in and out of focus? There had always been a blur in his life.

He brought Andrzej chess problems. That sometimes brought him briefly to life. But if Henning talked at all about the past, Andrzej drifted away.

Only Emma seemed really real to him. He clung to that. To her reality. To whatever she did or didn't do for him. Or to him. Henning could see there was a bitter taste in his mouth whenever he talked about her.

Most of the time, however, was downtime. Barren hours and small talk freighted with mutual disappointment. Quarter- or half-hours were spent with Henning's long body perched on a white enamel stool staring at the Pole's bony wide-apart knees two, three feet away, where his hospital gown scrunched up and behind, a useless sex hung. Others were spent in painful, patient silence.

As you might experience whilst out hunting. Being still and watchful. Just occasionally your quarry might give a small sign of life, the twitch of an ear, a nose raised to sniff the air. Then a little something might emerge without asking, an almost random fact.

One such fact was that on the afternoon of September 1, 1939, Emma had bicycled, not walked, over to where Andrzej then lived, which was the ground floor of a 'summer' villa along the Ourthes Canal.

Further details emerged—one at a time—over days.

That he had seen her coming. On a girl's bike. Seen her skirt spread on the lane, coming downhill. Seen the net over her back wheel and the basket in front.

Niemczyk said, I didn't know about the war. It started that morning. *J'avais pas de* TSF. He had no radio.

She asked for a glass of water. I used to grow cabbages in the garden.

Satisfied with that, Niemczyk fell silent again and Henning lit him a cigarette.

More hours passed. Whole days.

Circumstances were difficult. There was an orderly always in the room and a *gendarme* at the door. Andrzej was still sedated. A police psychiatrist, still wet behind the ears, made frequent 'observations'.

Andrzej didn't seem able to focus on any one thing for any length of time. He didn't like the bright light in his room, he didn't like the food, he didn't like the staff. He wanted to go home.

What for? Henning wondered. He was being looked after. Henning brought him cigarettes, books, papers, delicacies—all he would look at were the chess problems, and when Henning suggested they play a game, the Pole refused distractedly, his mind very much elsewhere.

Indeed, it might be, and was, days before Henning could get him to pick up the thread again.

Then, all he said was, I wondered who she was.

You gave her a glass of a water…said Henning helpfully.

She saw the piano.

Not the one you have now.

He ignored Henning.

I didn't ask her to sit down and play. I would rather she hadn't.

She was your student already?

Again Andrzej made no direct reply.

Henning's need to know had become something like a longing, and if anything, Emma became even more elusive when seen through Andrzej's eyes. She was or she wasn't his student? Was that the first time he saw her? As a girl in sailor blouse and straw boater riding downhill, tiny perfect beads of perspiration on her tall brow, an earnest look in her eye?

Nothing further emerged.

She was just out for a bike-ride? She got thirsty, saw a man working among the cabbages in his garden, asked for a drink of water and miraculously there was a piano inside?

Some days later, he tried again. He said, You were expecting her. She had been your student. The Pole shook his head stubbornly. You'd seen her at the Conservatory. You would have noticed her.

More days passed.

Then late one afternoon, Andrzej himself stumbled, like a man jumping across his own shadow, into another part of that September of 1939. Later. When the weather had turned Belgian, and the Russians invaded Poland from the East. When Kekes Tamas—as he said with a grim, unshaven smile—had to explain how the fascists were now allies. I hated him even then. Another exile. What his people were doing to my country.

Andrzej said, I could see her from my window. A man was waiting for her outside. She was mocking me. I could tell she was talking about me to him. You have no idea how sure she was. Of everything. Of Beethoven, of God, of…

Andrzej literally shrank on the edge of his bed, but forced himself to continue. Of *physical* things. Of her body.

The memory was frighteningly clear in his mind; it accounted for the anguish in his voice.

Every day they were getting closer to Warsaw.

Music? Henning asked. As though that might re-connect Andrzej. She walks in, she sits down at the piano—as in the ads Henning vaguely remembered from his childhood—and amazes?

On another occasion—even more depressed than usual—Andrzej lay back on his hospital cot, a bare bulb overhead, two long, bony hands joined by their tips over his eyes. He said, Please don't ask me about her.

Henning understood that what he meant was that it was painful to talk about Emma, as painful as not to think about her.

The police psychiatrist—in jeans, leaning back discreetly against the wall—said, It often happens after a suicide attempt. They feel guilty for being alive.

An idiot, Henning thought. Masquelier had been right. Andrzej's attempted suicide had been a last 'gift' to Emma, an attempt to protect her. Andrzej didn't feel guilty. He was afraid of what might come out of his mouth, of an obsessive memory that he couldn't control.

If you could leave us alone, Henning said to the young man.

Niemczyk lay there but some part of his mind was dreaming of Emma and 1939. It seemed not to be a happy dream.

At one point he saw Emma getting up from the piano and standing in the middle of the room, unpinning her straw hat, from under which flowed hair the color of bleached sand, then lifting the sailor blouse over her head and showing perfect pink apples while her skirt fell—apparently of its own accord—down into a puddle at her feet.

All he said was, It was me she wanted.

Henning remained silent, and odd little phrases—in no order at all—fell from his brain like shavings.

Yes, and did he lead her by the hand—this adolescent on the cusp of fifteen—to his awkward bed?

Why did she want me?

Briefly she was seen—naked again, very pale—parting the reeds by the water's edge and dropping into the water.

Henning could sense the intensity of the Pole's *watching*.

Then—Henning had to guess from fragments—someone had turned up. Perhaps the man in the photograph on whose arm, two years later, Emma was leaning.

She leaves the house one day and looking out of the window with mournful Polish eyes—always expecting the worst (Poles always lose)—Andrzej sees her look back and smile mockingly at him.

That's the last he saw of her and his recompense was that grand Pleyel that sat in his hovel. That too was a form of mockery, since she knows he can't play it half as well as she. Or, soon enough, at all.

Was that how it was? For once Henning was angry enough to actually touch the man, as though contact with the Pole's dry white skin could turn his own fingers into electrodes and himself into an oversized lie-detector.

Is that all some big lie? he asked Niemczyk.

No! I refuse to believe that! I can still feel her body! Leave me alone.

Andrzej's mind didn't grow any clearer, Henning explained to the *Commissaire*. Just more came out of it. All unconnected. He met with Masquelier after nearly every session with the Pole. With the notes he wrote up from fragments of Andrzej's delirium.

Or, as he said to the *Commissaire*, of the truth he is trying to avoid. It's the links. The links between different people, places and events have gone missing.

The Pole's memory was like a palimpsest, he said. Had the *Commissaire* read Alexandre Varille on Egyptian hieroglyphics? he asked. No? Well, Varille's theory was that you had to read Egyptian history backwards from the surface, layer by layer. It was not to be read in linear fashion, left to right, right to left, top to bottom or bottom to top. It was like Rome: one building put on top of an older, which in turn rested on one still older.

He was there. At the end, Henning said. He was not a *figurant*, an actor, a participant. He was an observer.

Masquelier said dryly, Our friend is the only one not afraid of Kekes. What do you make of that?

Nothing. To Andrzej, Kekes is irrelevant. If you look closely, I'll bet you find Nous Taad was not the only person who paid Niemczyk a small retainer. For forgetting. Pons too. There are two sets of people in there at the end and Andrzej is Berthe Kerkevelde's 'fourth man.' You know what I believe. I believe that murder is *always* personal, no matter what spin you put on it. Even the executioner knows his victim and has to bring himself to the drop of the gallows or the big switch for the chair by thinking, he *deserves* to be killed. That's always personal. Sensibilities vary.

But you think you know most of the story?

I know where it's lodged. In Andrzej's mind. There's a whole film there. Quite possibly of the last day too. But it's uncut, acetate, friable, dulled.

At one point Henning had come close, he was sure. The Pole had been talking about a 'secret area' that lay between two armies. In that secret area—without formal agreement, as if by chance—the two sides offer each other immunity. Andrzej seemed to be saying

I.I. Magdalen

that that space had come about as soon as Emma was shot and fell, when the cars drove towards them in the night and they—the four of them, Andrzej, Nous, Bernard and Kekes Tamas—could hear their engines and see their headlights.

Chapter sixteen

Arseen Conincq had not only retired, the past was no encumbrance. He retained in his consciousness just those things that touched him personally. He remembered his school days before the Great War (that is, in a completely different world); his beloved wife; and certain surrealists he had frequented between the wars (he was, he thought, at best an 'amateur' poet). In his old age—he was now ninety-one—his interests had become few, and specialized.

For instance, God, whom he had always taken seriously. Likewise the hybridization of roses and the music of certain nineteenth-century Belgian organists. He was the 'unofficial' organist of the Vrouwebasiliek in Tongeren and played there regularly.

Most of all, he was fascinated by the astonishing variety of individual greeds which he had observed during a long life as a notary, in the *cabinet* in Liège founded by his grandfather not long after Belgium became independent.

In some of these things he was, he knew, an amateur: an imperfect worshipper of God, a dabbler in horticulture, a reasonable musician. But about human greed, he was an expert.

There was no greed in Emma Hoofrad, he said. That had attracted him to the girl, and he'd known her parents well in his early artistic days. She had always seemed very pure. Not in a Church sense, meaning chastity. Rather that whatever she did, she stayed clean. That, he thought, was a matter of motivation. One could do bad things and smell of roses, but only when one did them for some far higher purpose.

He himself had always been absolutely transparent. Physically, that had made him into one of those very clean old men whose bodies looked held together by their clothes, by old-fashioned suits, with waistcoats, and shirts, stiffly starched at collar and cuff. He felt, literally, bodiless. His professional life was no different. Probity seemed so natural and so profitable to him that he could not understand why clients asked him to draw up peculiar documents, to declare (for taxes) sales of property at absurdly low prices or took perverse delights in concealing assets to avoid death duties (But how could that possibly affect you, my dear Johannes, when you will be dead?), who bought up Jewish property, who did not honor their parents' wills in regard to certain stipulated donations to the Church or charity—all those naturally devious things the greedy did. When God knew exactly what they were doing and would ask for an accounting.

He thought of the Hoofrads as being rather like himself.

He, Dr. Hoofrad, had been a scholar in jurisprudential matters and clear-hearted because he was more than a little abstracted from daily life. She, Isbel Kerkevelde, remained innocent as a child because the only thing that interested her was line and color and shape, and registering what her eye saw. And their only child was as pure-formed as a mountain stream because neither parent thought to teach her otherwise—if they thought to teach her at all!

He sensed two things about the Hoofrads. One, they could not survive in a greedy world. And on that score he was proved right. Thinking to please his wife and allow her to sketch further away from their home in Maastricht, Dr. Hoofrad had purchased a Delahaye, which he did not really know how to drive.

Two, Isbel was utterly unlike her sister Berthe, not to speak of his school-friend, poor Pim, who chose November 9th, 1918, to prove what a hero he was. Pim and Isbel were not survivors, Berthe was. When he drew up the adoption papers that sent the young Emma to her aunt, he knew it would not work out. Berthe would survive. He didn't see how Emma could.

Berthe took care only of herself.

Then he got a letter from an American who used Berthe's name by way of introduction. He—as his profession demanded—felt no bad blood toward Berthe or any of his former clients. Simply, he liked some more than others, and Berthe was not among his favorites. But, God willing, he would keep an open mind.

The letter had been respectably lawyer-like, but he didn't think he could help much. A notary's relations with his clients are held to the same standards of confidentiality as those observed in the confessional.

As it happened, he had quite forgotten his appointment with Mr. Forsell until the young man rang his bell.

Nonetheless, the young man made an immediate good impression on him. Henning had done his homework. He admired Conincq's three-manual organ, he liked his roses.

Once they had settled in the old man's study before a sturdy coffee pot and a plate of splendid chocolate pastries brought by his housekeeper, the young man threw himself on Conincq's mercies.

The young man said he'd been asked to perform a difficult task. It was something that had come about accidentally in his life. A curiosity about the *why*. What people are *really* like. It was something one can ask even about people one knew or thought one knew very well. One's parents, one's wife.

Arseen understood that without any problem. All people were mysterious; women simply more so. That is, you could describe them, you could detect their *types*, but their innermost thoughts were well hidden.

Emma? She had always seemed to him—perhaps because he had loved her with the tender affection of the childless man—straight as an arrow. Should have been called Daphne, he thought, or Laura for laurel, so lovely, so chaste. Did M. Forsell know the splendid Bernini in Rome, of Daphne—still fleeing—half turned into a laurel tree?

Henning said, Perhaps there is something I don't understand about the Flemish. Some admirable composure. Not at all river-creatures like Daphne. They seem so utterly domestic and discreet. It's not the picture I get of Emma.

Conincq still relished chocolate, and he relished talking about people. He made his biscuit last. And then the tiny thin cigar he lit when he'd finished his coffee. The conversation was just as pleasant to him.

There are different ways of fleeing. When Emma was a little girl—I should add, left totally footloose by her parents, often scampering about shoeless—she would come to our summerhouse in Oostend. She did nothing little girls are supposed to do. She was neither overtly affectionate nor did she sulk or say she was bored. She just made it plain she had quite enough locked up in her head to provide her with a very satisfactory day. No matter the weather, the beach, the waves, the tennis courts (and she was very good!).

When I say 'locked up', I mean that you never knew what she was doing, reading, studying, observing. She took it for granted for instance that if I played the organ, she was entitled too—even if her legs did not reach the pedals. She would take over from me and play from memory and I would never know where she had got it from or when she had memorized it.

That was (Conincq paused) before the war, before her parents' deaths. And even that she absorbed and internalized before the funeral—when the whole country was convulsed with grief over the loss of our Queen. Yes, yes, Uncle Arseen, she would say, I know what you're *trying* to say, you want to console me. But really I am already consoled, very *consoled*!

You can imagine how foolish an old man can feel, faced with a ten-year-old who has already worked out everything in her own mind.

You say, before the war, before her parents died. After that she changed in some way?

I.I. Magdalen

My wife and I would have liked her to come here to live with us—We had no children of our own. But of course, her mother's sister had the greater claim. She stopped coming for holidays. I really saw very little of her between 1936 and 1939. Though—at her request—I continued to look after her affairs. Her godfather, Bernard Pons, and I were old friends and we did what we could to accommodate her very firm will. Berthe, I think, was hurt. But she had struggles of her own and I expect she turned against her niece a bit.

Henning asked, She couldn't have chosen where she wanted to live?

Of course she could have! She chose not to. That was Emma all over. She was very sure of her position in the world and its rightness. That she should be adopted by Berthe was the right thing. As it was right that she should be free. Free as she'd always been.

I remember seeing her in 1937 in Luik while she was still at school. Just like her! She simply came to my office. She wanted to talk to me about her money.

She was twelve!

She was ageless.

And?

And nothing. I told her the money was prudently invested and would be at her disposal as soon as she turned twenty-one.

Which she never did. Who was the residual legatee? Her aunt?

I believe mainly institutions and charities.

It was the first imprecise answer Conincq had given him. But Henning preferred to continue.

You saw her again, then, in 1939?

Briefly. I made arrangements for her. She wished to leave her convent school in Mechelen and study music. I found a family for her to stay with and we hardly saw her.

She wasn't happy at her school?

No. She was a very pious child. She made up her own mind and became a Catholic. Though I am Catholic myself, I did not influence her. I don't think I could have. She decided such questions with due reflection, and once she had made her mind up, she was unshakeable. The same was true with music. She did what she wanted. I think she wanted to be independent.

If she wanted advice she went to you?

Or to Bernard. Yes, she preferred to deal with men.

Conincq fiddled with his coffee cup, hoping that his housekeeper would come in or that some other distraction would present itself. Because this sudden memory of Emma, of a meeting over forty years ago that he'd hardly thought about since, had suddenly become vivid.

Shown into his office by clerks who treated her as a little girl, she had appeared on the threshold as almost fully grown. He could see, even now, the crispness of the linen dress that stopped at her knees, and its color, a light beige that reflected the bleached sand of her hair which fell in tight ringlets from her high brow. She was so composed, her language so clear, so explicit.

He had been taken aback then. He was still taken aback now. If she was innocent, she was innocent in a way no girl her age had ever been when he was growing up. Those green eyes had settled on him, calmly and trustingly. But not as though he were a fond godfather, but rather as her notary, as the man who handled her property. She had said, I ought to know where I stand.

Hearing her again like that, he felt increasingly uneasy. The more he thought about her, the more real she became—as though she were sitting in the room with them.

He felt he was the only one left in the world who could remember her as she had been back then. It was a terrible responsibility. There were all these strands in her young life and he'd been laying them out for his guest, but what did he really know about them?

He dabbed at his forehead with a handkerchief, and heard, at some distance, his guest saying that perhaps he was tired, he would happily return at another time, or on another day.

Is something the matter? the American asked.

No, no. I was just thinking about Emma. You see, I haven't *had* to think about her for many years now. I mean, I have thought

I.I. Magdalen

about her often, but because I was asking myself things. Not because someone else was asking me. I express myself badly. What I mean is that having to think about her makes me feel accountable.

Of course Arseen could give a perfectly 'rational' explanation for this reluctance to carry Emma forward into the harder years of her adolescence, the bitter years of the war, the terrible scenes at the end.

Basically, he had known less and less about her. She was growing up. A 'secret' life had taken her over. It seemed to have removed her not only from his own life but from everyone else's, from the drab realities of life under the Occupation.

But what worried him far more—and far less rationally—was his feeling that he had been wayward (or even slothful) in preparing for this interview with the young American; he hadn't armed himself against such an open, untroubled curiosity. And where could it lead, if not to questions far more troubling than those of her girlhood?

He'd seen her again that year. During the winter. When the country desperately sought to remain neutral. She was still just fourteen and there she was before him again, in a felt hat that came down over one eye, a hat with a preposterous feather. And was she wearing (already hard to obtain, though not for rich young ladies) lipstick?

Perhaps not. But she was wearing an overcoat that had a fur collar.

He had felt then (and felt again now) that Emma, who seemed to have grown far taller, was moving away from him fast. That was why he didn't want to answer the American's questions any more. She had stepped, as she stepped into this room, into her pubescence, into a world of men.

It had been perfectly obvious, but he hadn't dared ask her about that new world. He felt he didn't have the right to (in the world in which he had grown up, such matters were private), but also there was the matter of how to approach such a subject with a girl who seemed to know so well what she wanted and what she would obtain. A girl, now that he saw her again, of almost unspeakable beauty—such that his wife, when Emma had left the following morning, felt it necessary to say, It will all end badly for her with those looks. With someone like that, you can't get close to her at all.

Of course, he'd heard from Bernard from time to time about these 'explorations' of Emma's. They were largely with men much older than herself and of very different backgrounds. But then he couldn't think of any young men who matched Emma.

If she had wanted to talk about them, surely she would have?

She'd given one name on that visit, that of a Pole to whom she wished to give a piano.

Looking him straight in the eye she said, A good one. He's a sad man.

A sad man and a *witness*. To the end.

Henning said, Did you see her when she came back to Liège at the end of the war?

Yes. Again briefly. With Bernard. No, she had not been especially perturbed. There was just something very different about her. Something damaged, Conincq said. Like the city itself.

Terribly thin was how she had appeared to him. Everyone was thin after five years of war and much barbarity. One could lose weight in one's mind and soul as well as in one's body. And the barbarity hadn't stopped with the war.

Conincq said, Of all the terrible things we all had in our souls at that time, revenge seemed to me both the most readily understandable and the most useless. Wasn't that what Christianity was about? Getting past the Old Testament idea of an eye for an eye and a tooth for a tooth?

She had no sense of what was going to happen to her? Bernard knew. You didn't?

Bernard wouldn't hurt a fly. If you mean did she know she was 'wanted' by some? Yes.

But she felt immune? Please. I need to know. She felt she had done nothing wrong?

She wasn't terrified. She was too beaten down for that, too much had gone wrong. I told her that Bernard and I would try to get her away. Possibly to France or England. She told me she couldn't go alone. She wanted to go with Kloosters. Her man.

They had met outside his office. In Bernard's apartment. On a Sunday.

And from there she had gone—on foot, as she'd been doing for weeks—to Andrzej Niemczyk. That, he couldn't tell M. Forsell. No one would. No one who knew.

Chapter seventeen

The undoing of Andrzej Niemczyk had been spectacularly quick. Some galloping cancers were like that. By the time Henning got around to searching the Pole's hovel and found the little blue book taped to the inside lid of the Pleyel grand, Andrzej's brain had cracked, hugely and almost totally—so how could you trust what he had painstakingly labeled 'My Confession'?

At the time of his final breakdown, Andrzej was in a convalescent home. The establishment was luxurious and Henning paid a pretty penny for it. And yet it had failed utterly. Or perhaps by then there was nothing that medicine could do.

One morning the Pole had woken up babbling. Babble, as in Babel, the Tower of. An outpouring of words in many languages—Polish, French, German among them—that made no sense.

The stalwart, buxom young nurse on duty that morning was on her first job. Already she had found the task of looking after the mentally disturbed disagreeable. If people were physically sick, there were medicines, reassuring doctors in white gowns, and if need be specialists and surgery; but with those who were sick in the head, what could you do?

She had disliked this patient from the start. He smelled. You supervised his bath, you made sure he used plenty of soap, you shaved him, he still smelled. It was an odor that came from somewhere deep inside him. It wasn't just old-man smell either. It was sicker than that. Most of the time he didn't talk. When he did, he ranted about Jews. She wasn't one, but the words he used were disgusting.

That was just the start. You couldn't persuade him to wear his pyjama bottoms. Though he hadn't done that with his Thing until that morning. But even before, if you wrestled him into his pyjama bottoms while he lay on the bed, he kicked them off and fondled his genitals. It didn't seem to give him any joy.

And because she dreaded going into his room, it fell to her to be the one who unlocked and opened the door to his room at half past six that morning.

It was a nasty shock. Her patient was stark naked and striding from one side of his room to the other. His right hand was fastened around his cock, which was small, swollen and red. He was shouting something that (to her) sounded like, 'Sixty, sixty, masturbate, masturbate, twice a night, I think of Her.'

She tried to lead him back to bed. He paid no attention. Ultimately, it was the babble that drove her from his room. That and the dreadful anger on his face, the distortion of his hollow cheeks, the way his mouth clutched and released words as his hand worked on his cock. He didn't seem to see her at all.

Finally, she fled down the main staircase (the 'home' had once been a rich industrialist's villa), after first having re-locked the door and laid her patient's breakfast tray just outside. Her instructions were to report any 'marked change.' Well, she told the Senior Night Nurse—who was about to go off duty—she'd been looking after him for a week without his saying more than a few words and now you couldn't stop him talking. And tugging his Thing. She said she didn't want to work in this sort of place anymore.

The Resident took his own sweet time getting there. The Senior

Night Nurse couldn't leave until her replacement came, and couldn't go upstairs just because the new nurse simply walked out. Procedures with a disturbed patient had not been observed.

Yes, Henning understood that the mad aren't nice. But even then, when they found the patient's room empty, why hadn't they raised an alarm? Why weren't the police notified until well past nine? They knew he was a suicide risk, they saw the open window that gave on to the balcony. Did they think—as the hill sloped up behind the villa—the fall from a second story room was not great?

They looked below, the Resident said. It was the first thing they thought of. But there was nobody there. They ransacked the villa without success. Then the gardens, which were surrounded by a high fence. He wasn't to be found. That was when they called the police.

Up the hill there was a back gate, a garden-gate, wasn't there? Could it have been left unlocked?

It had a padlock, the Resident said. The police found it locked.

Yes, but if it had been open, their patient almost certainly did get out that way. And locked it after him.

It was all very unsatisfactory, the police said.

Yes it was, said the *Commissaire*. His gesture took in the somber sky outside his windows as well as *la folie* and *le désespoir*. It's possible, Henning said, reading the Commissaire's gesture, his understanding of the nature of despair. In fact he had often thought of his father in those terms when he was younger.

But I'm not sure that despair—to the point of taking one's own life—is a form of madness. Suicide may also be the result of an entirely rational decision. Indeed there may be circumstances in which suicide is the *only* rational decision, Henning added gloomily, I suppose this time he succeeded.

Yes he did. Hanging from a tree. Like Judas.

There's always a first time. Isn't 'Judas' a bit hard on him? He didn't betray anyone.

He may have thought he had. And you call that 'rational'? By daylight, etc.

Emma H.

By daylight? Wearing only pyjama tops? To hang yourself from a tree in the back of a convent using bits of old cord you might find in anyone's potting shed? That doesn't strike me as rational.

Not to *our* rationality. Because we want to go on living. You want to retire and fish, or whatever it is pensioned-off *commissaires* do, and I have a lovely young wife waiting for me in Paris. But some people don't want to go on living. Some have very good reasons not to do so. Would the Church and the Law be so hard on our taking our own lives otherwise? Isn't despair, despairing of God's mercy, the greatest sin there is?

I feel nothing but deep sorrow for Andrzej. He had a rotten life. The kind to which death comes as a relief.

When he got back to his hotel, Henning felt spent. It wasn't healthy to be so often around the dead. At the same time, he felt— nothing new in that—that hotel rooms were lonely places. So instead of going to bed, he went off on a long walk, which took him down past St. Jean into the restaurant district. Even late at night it was filled with bars, men-only hotels, créperies, beer-joints and tight-jacketed and be-jeaned black girls, with the kind of pullulating life that people of Andrzej's generation couldn't even have imagined.

And didn't want, Henning also thought.

What Andrzej had wanted was Emma. And when she'd offered herself, that had been so inconceivable a gift he hadn't known what to make of it.

There were days when Henning thought that for Emma, Andrzej had been some noble act of charity—as with Catherine of Siena who drank pus from a suppurating wound. On others, he thought she walked in on him that day in 1939 because of pride. Because she wanted to punish herself for her pride. It could also be that she was just young and inconsequential. That like a normal girl of her age, she didn't think twice about what she was doing. That the opportunity was trivial, no one would ever know, she just took what she found and owned him forever after.

Then—when he read the little blue book—he knew what the

I.I. Magdalen

Pole had done at the end. Andrzej had tried to save her. That was why he'd been a witness.

And once again he'd failed?

Henning's answer was: Maybe. But he didn't fail with *her*. She knew what he tried to do for her. It may have been the last thing she knew. But that's still something pretty good to die with.

And yet, and yet. Cryptic, fragmented, elliptical, often incoherent, full of repetitive tics as though he hadn't fully understood the previous sentence, the little blue book had a still center and that center was Emma. It was a love story, the tale of a hopeless passion.

What any of it said about Emma herself was another matter. Possibly nothing. She was there in 1939, then she was gone and didn't come back until six years later. And when she did come back, it was far too late to save anything. For her, or for Andrzej.

The so-called 'Confession' must have been written in the few days between his first meeting with the Pole and Andrzej's arrest. Mlle. Giedroyc, the daughter of a distinguished poet, both deciphered and translated it for him. She said that though it was obviously the product of a disturbed mind, the Polish of the text was correct and sometimes even elegant. The author, she said, was an educated man.

It would seem best simply to let Niemczyk speak for himself on those matters that relate directly to Emma H. and his own tortured existence.

Chapter eighteen

My troubles began when I had to leave Poland. The reason I left Poland I shall leave for the end of this account. My father was a merchant in Lodz. He had a haberdashery business in the center of town. He killed himself when his business failed in the hyperinflation of the post-war years. I was then thirteen.

With the few possessions we had not sold, we took the train down to Çzestochova. There my mother prayed to the Virgin on her knees and implored Her help. And there she met my stepfather at the communion-rail. She always considered this a miracle.

We took the bus with him and settled with his mother in Pszczyna. He worked in the mines nearby.

It was a very considerable change of life and my mother did not last long under those conditions. My stepfather was, however, devoted to her. She had artistic aspirations, which were stifled in Pszczyna, and he decided that, as I would never follow him into the mines, I should study, and I was more than willing, in order to escape life among people with whom I had no affinity.

Emma H.

Thanks to our parish priest, I was sent back to Lodz. This priest convinced my stepfather that I had a gift for music.

I did have a certain gift. But it was not sufficient to sustain me in the grueling work of the Conservatory. Music was a torture, practice on the piano was torture. I sensed my lack of aptitude. A lamp stood precariously, very precariously, on a pile of sheet music on top of the piano. With a Jewish shawl over it. The rest of the room was dark and girls walked by. Looking up, they could see my light. I was in there thinking about those girls and not about music.

My stepfather *wouldn't* understand that I didn't want to be a musician, that I didn't want to play scales all day, that I wasn't good enough.

I wrote him that now that I was back in Lodz, I knew what I wanted to do. I wanted to become a shopkeeper like my real father. I would have a shop in the center of Lodz with a brightly lit window. A fine shop. And all the girls who walked by would come in for me. He said I just needed to work harder. If I didn't pass my exams, I was to come home and he would find work for me in the mine.

I did just manage to pass my exams at the Conservatory. No favor was shown to Christians or the lower orders generally. Jews took all the prizes and gentlemen's' sons and daughters received preferential treatment from the faculty and the Director.

I gave one public concert at a sporting-club, to which I invited my stepfather.

It was a catastrophe. I forgot the music and made mistakes even with pieces I knew well and had been playing for years. At first the audience only tittered. Then they laughed. And finally, they walked out. I never saw my stepfather again.

I took my small cachet and got on the train for Berlin, resolved never to play the piano again.

It was at this time that I met S., as I shall relate later.

I no longer have any nostalgia for Lodz or any other place on earth. Ever since I decided to take my own life, I am very calm, and I am able to pass over without imploring anyone for pity (as my mother pleaded with the Virgin in Częstochova), all the difficulties

I.I. Magdalen

a penniless and untalented youth in his twenties could have in the mid-1930s, especially a Pole. We are a despised race.

In the several cities I passed through, drifting westward as we Poles do—like our Chopin, I think we have a fixation on Paris—I survived only because I had a gift for figures. If I had not drunk too much, I might have been a reasonably successful bookkeeper. In Dresden, in Prague, in Mannheim, in Köln. But instead of having my own shop in Lodz, I finished up in Liège keeping the books for a number of small companies.

I would regularly get fired: for not showing up (drink) or for making mistakes (a growing confusion in my mind).

One of these companies was owned by Nous Taad, who at the time had a small trucking business and wasn't yet a big shot. Thus I was in a position to know a great deal about him and his crooked ways. As he was one of those who fired me, I suppose the police will soon find out about our relations and try to connect me with his death, which was well merited. He had many enemies.

They went back to the war-years. Back then, survival for a business meant cheating the Germans, the law, the government, one's friends, as well as one's enemies.

I had ample reason to seek revenge on him: not just for dismissing me from my stupid but necessary little job but also for his behavior towards the girl.

If anyone finds and reads this, it will be obvious what Emma was to me. And to others who were just as dazzled by her as I was. But less disarmed.

I have been questioned about her. Others have been questioned too. That is why I write this. Soon no one will be able to bully me about her.

The summer of 1939 was a superb summer for anyone who did not know what was coming. The sun shone brilliantly, and even a grimy town like Liège basked in it.

But for me—someone who had no future at all—that summer was Emma. She was my fate and my destiny. Had I opened my shop, in Lodz or here, she is the girl who would have walked in for me.

With her, no one could have any idea of what he was getting into. No man could have. Anyone could see her. Everyone saw her. She was that extraordinary, and she wanted to be noticed. How could you help noticing her?

I had no idea she was thirteen. She didn't look thirteen (she turned fourteen just before Christmas). I thought she was sixteen or seventeen. There was nothing of the child about her except the look of innocence she wore on her face and body. And there was nothing innocent about her except that look.

(It is strange to think that I can write of her with this sort of distance, when she was for so long the source of my illness and distress. Perhaps what I am about to do was what I should have done long ago in Lodz, as my father had, instead of meeting S., instead of leaving Poland. I should have allowed myself to be buried in the soil that made me.)

When I first saw her she was hurrying out of shops, always carrying parcels. She would put the parcels in a big basket on her handlebars and cycle off. Somewhere. What anyone saw was a tall girl with golden hair, very calm green eyes, and a terrible self-possession. I say 'terrible' because it occurred to me even then, before I knew her, that nothing and no one could stand in her way. The shopping, the way she was dressed, the way she walked into or out of a shop (what should have been my shop!), you knew she had money. No, you knew she was rich. And the rich will always prevail. Then she was beautiful in so paralyzing a way that even striking up an acquaintance with her seemed out of the question. She belonged in a princely world.

But we were all frogs and none of us was a prince in disguise.

Her bicycle came up next to mine along the Rue St. Gilles. I did not dare look. But I saw bright colored strings on her back wheel that kept her skirt from the spokes. A summer skirt. It was a long and light summer skirt. She pedaled without effort. She did everything without effort. After that time, I seemed always to be on the same road at the same time as her, but I was sure she never noticed me—a penniless clerk the wrong side of thirty and neither well-dressed nor unusual in any way.

Then I followed her one day, which is what I think she expected me to do.

I can't say her presence at that place or that time was part of any design of hers or that she had the slightest interest in me. She was where she was because that was the kind of person she was. And when I pedaled after her, she took it as her expected tribute.

She had to know what I was doing, however. Where we went, early that summer, was well beyond the busy center of the city, out into a district of breweries and warehouses.

Eventually, she stopped and stepped off her bicycle and into a sort of hall where there was a political meeting going on. At least I was given a handbill as I went in, which she wasn't. She seemed to know the two young men at the door and just walked in as though she belonged there. A girl of her class! Of her elegance!

Once inside, I stood at the back, though I had eyes only for her. There was a man speaking up on the platform and a red banner hung over his head with a hammer and sickle, from which I concluded that the speaker was a communist agitator, of whom there were many in Liège at the time. I didn't understand that much French then, but the speaker, who looked like a rooster, with reddish-blond hair cut short except in the middle and very bad eyes behind thick glasses, was compelling. I could see that she knew him as well as many others in the crowd, almost all of whom were in suits and wore caps.

I left because the speaker talked about Russia and revolution and I don't like change or Russians, and the Bolsheviks, as any Pole knew, were Russian pigs and Jews.

I suppose I was disappointed in her. Why would she be interested in such people?

The speaker was Comrade Kekes.

I tried to forget about her, but of course that was impossible.

I have always been a compulsive masturbator and that summer

Emma H.

was when she became the girl I thought of while gratifying myself. I made love to her in every detail: her tiny ears, her delicate mouth, her small but perfect breasts. I saw that high brow of hers bent over me and her ringlets swaying over my stomach.

It would have been all right with me if she'd remained the object of my fantasies and no more. The same was true of S.

Instead she came to the house I was staying at. There was a not very good piano in my house, and at that time I sometimes thought I could still make a modest living teaching—young ladies I hoped—so I'd been practicing a little.

The woman who rented me the ground floor wanted a man in the house. Her husband was dead. He was the one who'd played the piano. She was always hanging around wherever I was, bringing me things, asking me if I wanted to share her dinner, she'd made this or that.

She was leaning out the window when Emma came up on her bicycle. I said something stupid like, It may be for a piano lesson, so that she wouldn't interfere. Emma looked at me with a cool smile.

After that, she came every weekend and she sat down at the piano and ran through her Hanon and Czerny and the like. It's not hard to imagine how I felt. It was her sheer inapproachability. She played the piano as she looked. That is, she was so perfect in body and mind and expression that it was uncanny; I really and truly thought she'd invented herself. Well, she played the piano like that. As if the instrument and even those dreadful exercises had just been invented and there were nothing to it, that anybody could do it. Just hearing her play a Schubert sonata—easy technically, but emotionally miles beyond most interpreters—was a chilling experience. Elfin, morbid, playful, melancholy.

Where did it come from? *She* hadn't gone through years of torture under a lamp covered with a Jewish shawl in a Lodz attic. Oh no! It just came to her.

She was not only too beautiful for me, she had all the real gifts that had been denied to me and to someone like S.

Yet she wanted me.

I.I. Magdalen

I do not expect to be believed, but it is true. I could sense it. She wanted to be touched. That was where it started. She would put her hand next to mine.

She came on the first of September when Poland was invaded.

Stupidly, I had cut my hair for her and bathed. I still couldn't touch her.

On that memorable day, I lost my head. When she had given me the news—I knew Poland would be brought to its knees—she sat down at the table and looked at me for a long time without saying anything. How can I explain it? She was radiating. She was like the summer. What did she expect of me? When I said nothing, she went out to her bicycle—I thought she was leaving—and brought back a volume of Schubert four-hand music, which she propped up on that rotten old out-of-tune piano and asked whether I wanted to play the treble part or the bass.

How did she even know I played?

I had never played half so well, not a tenth so well. Everything fitted easily. My hands did what they were told. When we had finished the one in F minor, she smiled at me without a word, then she went outside in that glorious sunshine and lay down on the lawn, which was really more like a meadow that ran down to the river. What young girls are expected to do, she did. Not young girls, young ladies. The fancy had taken her. If young ladies like Emma want to run down to the river and leap into the water, they do. Naked. Leaving fine clothes on the bank.

Young ladies like Emma are not acquired; they do the acquiring.

The war came on ever so slowly and Emma went ever so quickly and abruptly: to a new and different world. We saw the defenses go up and soldiers in tin hats patrol the Albert Canal. My landlady threw me out of her house because of my drinking and in mid-winter I went back into the city where, like many others, including Taad, but on a much smaller scale, I made a still smaller living stockpiling scarce goods and selling whatever Taad gave me to sell.

I was on fire and there was nothing to quench it with. No Emma, no bicycle, no slender skirts.

I went everywhere I might see her, I even made friends (of a sort) with Kekes, who had moved on to 'greater responsibilities' (meaning more Russian *merde*) in Brussels.

He was a liar. He said he'd made love to Emma often. He described her as a camp follower. The idea of revolution attracts aristocrats, he said. It was a way of defying their families. He said I should stop working with Nous Taad, he was going to come to a bad end. He also told me 'the Hoofrad girl' had an aunt who was a fascist.

Hoofrad? I didn't even know who she was until he told me. I'd never thought of Emma having a family of any kind. We didn't talk. That is, sometimes she would talk, coaxingly, while anything I wanted to say got stuck in my throat. I had no idea what she was like.

In fact, now that I look back on that period in my life, I don't think I had understood *anyone*, but Emma least of all. When circumstances are all against you, as they were with me, whether in Lodz or here in Liège, you can lose your bearings. What you know to be real no longer seems so. I spent more and more time in the little house that Taad had bought and which he let me use while I worked for him and which I think he forgot all about.

At night, I thought about Emma and made love to her by myself.

I didn't see her again until April of 1940, when the thought of killing myself began to fill my mind, the way maggots fill a corpse.

To prepare myself I wrote about S.

Thinking about S. reminded me of my mother, of our leaving Lodz, of my mother praying in Częstochova (because I had kept the picture of the Virgin which she had given me back then), and I thought that before going I would pay a visit to God and explain to Him, and to his Holy Mother, that it was all up with me.

This strange and painful meeting came about because of the missionary efforts of Father Krzysztof, a Franciscan friar from Krakow.

I.I. Magdalen

He entered our lives (by 'our lives' I mean what was left of the lives of the Poles whose habitual hell-hole was Elizabeth's) at that peculiar, unstable time—when it was all but certain that within days or weeks at the most the Germans would be marching into Belgium—thanks to his own spirit and because of Bernard Pons.

I did not know then that Pons was Emma's godfather. I know that when the money was on the table and the stakes at their highest, he was one of us.

Back then, there were still young men like me in Elizabeth's smoky bar by the canal and the main locks, once a bargee's drinking-hole. Soon (but for myself and one or two others) all these young men were sent off to work in German factories, while the older men, retired from or disabled by the mines, were left behind, and turned their attention and talents to smuggling and the black market, which the barge-men stoutly supported.

We were riff-raff and marginals and drunks, and Father Krzysztof was determined to remind us that we were all also Catholics. To me, he was a lifeline. A bustling, bristling, energetic man, he had fought against the Russians in the 1920 war and had escaped the German Blitzkrieg in 1939 only because he was on holiday in Rome.

It was with him that I went to mass at a convent where he acted as confessor.

There she was, kneeling on a *prie-dieu* at the front of the congregation, a white veil over her fair hair, but her body and demeanor unmistakable, absolutely still and apparently praying with tranquil fervor, as prayer should be. Next to her were two men: one was tall and strikingly handsome in a cadaverous way - Bernard. He later became a resistance leader and for many years has helped (foolishly) to keep me alive. The other man was shorter and more compact. He was conspicuous because of the Rexist uniform he wore. This was "Henri" (Henryk) Kloosters, one of the inner circle of the Rexists.

In 1940, all I could feel was envy. These men flanked my Emma, not me. All thoughts of God fled my mind. I had been used and then discarded: for reasons I knew all too well, that I was inadequate, without distinction or talent, pathetic. I hated her, too. She had undone me once, had brought music and something like love, and then vanished.

She knelt there as though none of this were her doing: abandoning me just as she had abandoned her elegant clothes on the bank of the river. As though life were a form of accommodation to the basic fact of her beauty, her wealth, and her talent. As though she were powerless to do anything with what she hadn't earned but had been given her. And still no more than fourteen.

I hated God, too, then—for bringing into the world a child who wasn't a child at all, but an Eve who betrayed everyone she met; who made out that she loved in order to abandon, and who did abandon her gift for music; who stopped being what she was, a girl—a mere girl—to become someone infinitely more dangerous.

Then I saw her in the illustrated papers. On Klooster's arm. By then she had become a notorious woman. The Germans had come. (I don't know how Pons must have felt. Presumably, he was torn apart by her defection to the Occupying Power. Nor do I know what led Emma in that direction. It was hard to think of her as just a girl in love.)

The war dragged on.

I did not kill myself then. I don't know why not. Perhaps I simply expected to be killed and, ironically, wasn't.

Early in 1945, I received a postcard, posted in Berlin and sent to me at Elizabeth's, and signed E.H. It said, 'Need help.'

I would have helped her if I'd been in any condition to, but I had spent the winter of 1943–4 in prison (arrested for black-marketeering and ordered on release to report to the Labor Commission for 'reassignment', the euphemism for able-bodied foreign workers sent to Germany). The German offensive in the Ardennes that winter and the subsequent fallback of their army saved me.

Emma did not seek me out, but I heard from Father Krzysztof that he thought she had passed through the convent, to which she had apparently been a generous donor.

All he knew about her wartime history was that it had been

I.I. Magdalen

full of vicissitudes, that she had been in Berlin (and perhaps raped by the Russians), that they—she and Kloosters—had decided it was safer to split up and meet abroad (I heard he had reached Spain eventually). Father Krzysztof told me that some sort of 'court' was trying to put her on trial. He said the communists in Brussels had sought her extradition from the British forces on charges of treason and collaboration.

It was alleged, long ago, before she was forgotten, that I betrayed her to the resistance. The accusation may have been made by her aunt, Berthe Kerkevelde, who had fled the country as soon as Brussels was liberated (the previous summer). The aunt was thought to be traveling to the Holy Land.

I deny this. It is an absolute falsehood put about by Kekes and the communists in their attempts to dominate the French part of Belgium after the war ended. Kekes had every reason to distract attention from his own betrayal of his companions in the party. Nous Taad had proof of this betrayal. He kept his 'proof' for years and Kekes could never harm him or his business.

I will be very brief about Emma's 'execution'. I only heard about it by accident from a Pole who knew Kekes. By the time I arrived at the old union hall where I had first seen her with Kekes and his Bolshevik companions the so-called trial was over. I was told that she had been taken by the three resistance officers (Kekes, Pons and Taad) for execution. Where, they either did not know or were unwilling to say.

How had they gone? Someone shrugged—obviously it was a matter of no concern to them—and said they thought they'd gone in one of the Public Works trucks. Kekes had access to them. Was he driving? I asked. They sent me to the devil. I wasn't one of them.

They made a joke of it all. Did I want to see the fascist bitch shot? Was I looking for excitement?

I don't know how, but I had an inkling Taad rather than Kekes would have done the organizing, and I remembered once meeting with him for a shipment of light bulbs somewhere deep in the woods east of the city where he said he had a hunting cabin. I remembered the old truck lumbering up a hill, and rows of pine trees, an abandoned quarry. But how would I get there in time to do anything about it?

Her aunt? She wasn't there. The police? What would they care?

Then I thought of Father Krzysztof. There was a telephone at the back of the hall, and I explained to the priest what was going on. I said I was only guessing. He said he trusted in God.

A half hour later we were at the main road where it crosses the steep climb up to Taad's property. We turned off our lights, parked off the highway down below, and started up. It was very dark inside the woods, but we could hear voices.

Father Krzysztof went up through the wood on one side of the driveway, I went up the other, asking myself what I was doing there, knowing I didn't want Emma dead, only punished.

What I saw is very clear to me, even all these years later.

To one side was the little house I'd been to with Nous Taad; in the middle was the track that led through the woods to the quarry; on the other side was a van belonging to the Department of Works. Closest to me were Taad and Pons, who were arguing about something. A few steps in front of them, Kekes held Emma by the arm and was pushing her up the track. He was holding the only light, a flashlight. It was focused on the ground in front of himself and Emma.

Suddenly, all three men stopped as though they'd heard someone. Kekes let go of Emma's arm, but she continued walking at the same pace. Then I too, and perhaps Father Krzysztof also, heard what they'd heard: the sound of several cars coming up the highway from Liège, cars slowing down, cars turning, cars beginning to climb up towards us. What should we do? Intervene now? Wait? Yell out?

I let Father Krzysztof's God decide.

At that point, I got a last glimpse of Emma. She too turned around. She wore a simple dress and a scarf about her head. She looked thin and ghostly, as if already dead, but also, in some way that I recognized from that summer of 1939, totally composed. It was as if she had done the deciding for us, and she did not want anything to happen that wasn't already decided. Her hands were at her side, her long legs were whiter than the rest of her. She said nothing. She didn't move at all.

Then Kekes' flashlight was turned off. Looking behind me, I saw the lights of the first car approach, reaching only the tops of the pines. There was a flurry of activity along the track, I think three, perhaps four shots rang out, and the cars coming up the hill stopped and turned off their lights.

My stepfather had told me once that during the Great War in which he'd fought on the front in Bukovina, there were certain times and places, arrived at completely spontaneously, without planning or foresight, in which two armies, facing one another in trenches or woods, or especially in valleys between hills, mutually accepted that the space between them was free of fire. These became empty spaces, a kind of guaranteed no man's land. They could be used to escape, collect the dead, to smoke a cigarette, for any normal human reason.

The same thing happened up there by Taad's lodge.

Kekes, Taad and Bernard Pons melted away into the woods; Emma presumably lay on the track, dead; Father Krzysztof and I hurried away back to our car; as did, presumably, the *gendarmes*.

I am reasonably certain the good father had called them and told them where we were going before he picked me up. I supposed then they were the ones who found Emma's body.

That's all I know about it and the matter was not raised again until Emma's aunt published her letter in the local newspapers. All of us went back to our homes as though nothing had happened.

I write and sign this so it can be known that I will die without ever having revealed Emma's secrets. Some of these—What she did during the war and how she survived Russia and at what cost—I do not know myself. Nor have I any insight into her secret life (her music, her God, her love). I leave it to Bernard—as far as I know the only man she wrote to or talked to about herself—to 'explain' her. As he can (so long as he remains alive)—if he wants to, explain what happened that night—that I myself only realized when I heard that Nous had been killed—I have said nothing more than the truth as I saw it.

Chapter nineteen

The light had gone outside, drooling away to somewhere more interesting or to where light more properly belonged. Henning got up, lit the candle that was in the vodka bottle on the table, took it with him, and went into the other room. Where was the rest of Andrzej's confession, the part relating to 'S.'? It must be here, he thought. Because Andrzej had never had a life elsewhere. And now, didn't have a life at all.

He opened the lid on the Pleyel, ran his fingers along the keyboard on which Emma had played long ago. A nasty, musty draft made the candle gutter. Everything here was out of tune.

Emma's photograph stared at him. It felt odd to him to have come to know so much about a girl without a single word of hers in his head. Not a scrap of paper. Not a joke, an endearment, or anything she'd ever said. Everyone talked about her; she said nothing.

He picked the picture up and stared at it. A dead girl in a straw hat with nothing to say. He picked up the other picture. Of the hanged man when young and 'pretty' and a girl handing him a bouquet.

Both photographs had mysterious emanations but, unlike the Ghost Dancers his Pa had told him about, these emanations were all of defeat and despair.

Me too, Henning thought. I don't believe in salvation, I don't believe the waters will rise and wash the world away. Or that the buffalo will once again roam the prairie. And these two—Andrzej and Emma—were linked in some sin of despair. Where was the God who should have saved them?

He felt kinship with these two. Their kinship with himself, his with his Pa.

All four of them had dark parts in their lives that they could not readily share with anyone else. The Blue Book was hidden in the piano, 'S' was hidden somewhere, Emma was hidden behind her beauty. Essentially, they were solitary, and that made them mysterious and untouchable to others.

He didn't think many people led secret lives as a conscious choice, but many did so out of necessity. Andrzej, Andrzej's father, his own Pa, his Pa's cousin Harald. After Viet Nam and the Congo and Rhodesia, Cousin Harald had come home and made the most precise arrangements to blow his brains out. He had posted on his garage door, 'DO NOT COME IN. CALL FOR AN AMBULANCE.' There had been no one he could really talk to, because no one had been through what he'd been through. And what was the point—after living an extreme life—of living a trivial one?

Secrets destroyed friendships and even love. They raised obstacles even between the most intimate.

He put both pictures in his raincoat pocket and left. With no doubt at all that Niemczyk had meant the photographs to be *his*. They had been addressed to him.

It was only when he got back to his hotel and took the pictures out of his pocket that he realized that the back of one of the pictures—that of Andrzej on the fatal night of his debut—had been taped to the frame. Even before opening it up, he knew 'S' was there.

When he'd read it, he felt unable to pass judgment on the

I.I. Magdalen

Pole. He wasn't a bad man. He was a displaced person. Displaced inside himself.

Possibly that was what Emma had seen, and briefly loved him for, with that kind of headlong love-abandonment that marks adolescence. Someone who could stand there in a dark wood and despise the men who were about to kill her would have divined a like spirit in Andrzej. He'd worn the same pair of corduroy trousers and the same shirt all his life; and worn the same soul and the same life. As she'd worn her beauty.

If only she'd done as Andrzej had done. Set herself down on paper.

This is what he read.

my confession

Why did I leave Poland?

I killed a young woman, a schoolgirl. I didn't intend to, nor did it happen by accident.

She had no talent, no beauty, no prospects. It seemed she should be dead. In a way, instead of me.

I have always referred to her as S. She is available for scrutiny in this photograph. She is the girl handing me that pathetic bouquet of flowers. The whole audience had gone, but she stayed. She stayed behind just to be *nice*. The worst insult of all.

She said, do you want me to walk home with you?

I said, you should go home.

She said I shouldn't be sad. Sometimes bad things happened. As an example, she said that right where we were walking, barely a hundred years before there had been impenetrable forests.

I told her to shut up and go home. I said, Now it is the ugliest and longest main street in Poland. Can't you see there are no forests here any more?

If we'd been in Warsaw, I'd have pushed her off the bridge. Instead, she slipped as she ran to get on the last trolley, which was crowded with people going home from the center. She thought I had taken hold of the belt around her coat to hold her back. Perhaps she thought I'd like a goodnight kiss. Therefore, she slipped, and because I was right behind her, she fell under the wheels. People shouted.

After having answered questions from the policeman, I went back to my room and stole some money from my landlady. I knew she kept the rent money in a jar in her kitchen.

I took nothing else. I took the first train West.

Henning could see him writing these dreadful things in the room from which he'd just come: bent over the lid of Emma's piano, his hand shaking.

Perhaps this strange *Nachlass* of words left behind like some long-lost bank deposit had some truth to it. Or was true in one way and not in another. These things—the desirous Emma, the executed Emma—could well have happened, but did they happen the way Andrzej said they did? Were these confessions what the Pole wanted others to believe, or were they the way Andrzej would have liked things to have happened?

It was possible Andrzej didn't try to save Emma. Instead he was the one who betrayed her. He didn't kill the harmless S., but he wished he had.

Dreadful thoughts to have about another human being. Crime was not always casual. Sometimes crimes occurred because the occasion presented itself.

He sat on the edge of his bed, tired, dismayed, angry with Andrzej—Who asked him to tell his stories?

He thought, I've got to do something about this whole business, it's got to come to an end or I'll just go on turning round and round. Every path I've pursued so far brings me to people who give me information but suppress the truth: Tante Berthe, Conincq, Andrzej, Masquelier. The man left you plenty of clues. Give it a week. Berlin: what Emma was doing there. Who Kloosters is and what happened to him. Why the British turned Emma over and who made that decision. Simple, accessible, factual things. Not motivations. Not the last words of madmen. Nor the lies of interested parties.

Eventually, he fell into an uncomfortable sleep.

Chapter twenty

It was a mean, inverted autumnal evening, with the dark and wet below and a pearly sky above. Wind and rain stripped trees of their leaves, and the air was thick with their smell. Six weeks he'd been in Belgium, and it seemed that all about Henning, leaves were being burned; and drenched; then burned again.

He'd sat in the Liegois a half-hour around seven with the *Commissaire*. That had been dispiriting. All he'd learned was that Masqulier had taken Kekes in for questioning. That's all. There was no urgency of any sort. So Taad was dead. Henning said, Shouldn't we give him a moment's thought? Does nobody have a good word for him?

The *Commissaire* said, I don't mean that it's not my duty to examine the unlawful death of anyone. A prostitute is knifed down by the canal. That I can understand. It's human. But Taad? Why expend a lot of energy on the death of such an up-to-date man, vain, self-serving, interested in money and the small change of power? It was to have him be *that* that his mother labored to bring him into the world and brought him up to be clean and a good boy? So that he could never have an idea or a feeling? Not even for his secretary?

No, I think he was used up in the *maquis*. That was his moment of glory. I had a Jewish boss when I was young. He would have said Taad was a '*Macher*'. A fixer. *Santé*, he said, draining his glass and getting up to go.

Well, one thing Henning had learned about Belgium. It was a well-hidden place, fickle as weather, intricate in history, deadly in its rivalries. Which he guessed was about right. Small countries had to be like small towns; the smaller they were, the more complex.

When Henning had gone, Masquelier walked back to his office and called Pons. He said, I think we have to talk.

Bernard hurried over. He too was anxious. Just how long could Masquelier keep Kekes in custody? Two of the five other men who'd been at Taad's hunting lodge that night were dead. That left three. And Father Krzysztof was now a very old man, and frail. Tenacious as he was, he wouldn't last forever. Of those, all but one—the one who'd never known and was all the more dangerous for that—had managed to keep their secret. And how many people managed to go to their graves with their secrets?

Will I be able to? he asked himself. If I do, that means Kekes gets off scot-free. That shouldn't be allowed. Not when human accounts were being drawn up, not with God looking on.

Alas!—as he saw walking into the *Commissaire*'s office—Masquelier was another tired old man. He was no longer the young inspector whose police cars had headed into the hills at the very last possible moment.

Bernard said as he shook the *Commissaire*'s hand, What do we do now? All of us are many years past our best days. We do not glow with health like M. Forsell. Taad was right. We should have shot Tamas back then when we had the opportunity. We were a few feet away. No one would have known. I had my gun in my hand, Nous had his. We had half agreed.

The *Commissaire* didn't react. He just shrugged and nodded. This was old business between them, though they hadn't talked about Emma for years.

The *Commissaire* said, To be young has a meaning only when

one is young. Only when one imagines one can do anything. Most people wouldn't want to go back unless they could do things differently.

Bernard replied, I can't feel *sorry* for the person I was in 1945. What would be the point of that? Nor am I proud of it. There's no clock that measures morals. *Autres temps, autres moeurs.* But at my age, knowing what I know now, for nothing in the world would I be that young man playing games of patriotism and revenge, all of them very foolish. You know what happened. You were there and things would be quite different if you hadn't been. We were lucky. I saw that. The war was at last over. I could put a shell on my back and, as a turtle withdraws his head into his carapace, I hid myself in my mind. Archives proved good for mental health. Along with deeds and transfers of property, affidavits, dispositions, grants, records of favors granted, there are also lives to be perceived there. But in the abstract. They are no threat to me. I don't want to die with a lie on my conscience.

Masquelier said, Unlike you, I just went on doing what I'd always done. I didn't and still don't have a shell to retire into. Just an ordinary retirement about twenty-seven weeks and four days away.

You're less ordinary than you make out.

No, I'm probably more ordinary than you imagine. There are few fine distinctions in my work.

You don't want to forget the whole affair?

I would love for it to be forgotten, but not for me to forget it. Didn't you once tell me that there was no such thing as the history of today? That it was impossible? That the nearest you could get was a hundred or more years ago? Well, here—Masquelier said, dropping an envelope in front of Bernard—is the proof of your sense of history. That not enough time has lapsed since the war in which we played our games and you say you want to forget.

What's this?

A missive from Mlle. Pascale, the departed M. Taad's secretary. Stolen goods if you will. It's what Nous kept in his safe for protection.

Bernard looked at the envelope without touching it.

Don't be afraid, the *Commissaire* said. It's what we've known all along. It would seem that in the last days, the Gestapo forgot to destroy *everything*. Or quite possibly it means—as you and I always thought—that Nous had intimate contacts with the Germans.

Though not so intimate as those of our friend Tamas. You don't want to see it with your own eyes? It contains a list of payments they made to Kekes. It contains a list of those companions whom he sold to the Gestapo. It's for the contents of this envelope that Kekes killed Nous and went to his apartment to break into his safe.

Why do you want me to read them?

I don't care if you read them. I care that you *keep* them. They cannot stay here. I will be gone and they could 'disappear'.

And they shouldn't?

Like Emma H. you mean?

Yes. The same way.

Then take them, Bernard. Take them. You have sealed archives.

Pons pushed the envelope into a pocket and thought of Emma's letters and her desire for anonymity. Her need to be forgotten and buried. Once she had said she never wanted anything else even as a child. That it should all be over.

Chapter twenty-one

The hotel dining room was cold and empty. Henning sat there, an old customer by now, and ate and drank mechanically. Alone. As he'd been in many places and many hotels. Alone and telling himself that when you came right down to it all this ceaseless kind of prying he did was a sort of punishment. For a lifetime of hiding himself and his own life.

He felt surrounded by unhappy lives and meaningless deaths. He was to say that to Bernard the next day.

It's awful. *They're* awful. People like Kekes. Just as well he had no child. Ideologues make lousy husbands and fathers, especially the latter. As though they didn't want children who would grow up to live in the world they were planning. And businessmen make lousy lovers. And artists? Do you think it's a generation thing? You can say I was lucky to escape those times. But I might get to understand them. Isn't that more likely than that you might understand me?

Henning thought a lot about that.

He couldn't say he understood his father, but there was *no* chance of his Pa understanding him.

Meanwhile, Pons sat at his usual place. Before him, steaming on his plate, was a mountain of lamb kidneys baked in their fat, with a slope of buttery mashed potatoes below, richly mixed with blood and gravy. Yes, he thought all those things. Or he had thought them at one time or another. He wasn't surprised that the American felt tormented. Emma had been tormented. That's what he should have replied to the *Commissaire*—that to be young is to be tormented.

Eventually there is resolution, Bernard answered. That is what God offers in human affairs, a way of coming to an end.

If, of course, one has the grace. And if one can come to a good end.

Frankly, the American made him feel terribly old, and age was doubly loathsome to Bernard. Over here, death was coming his way. Over there were the young, pushing and shoving and striving.

There was a barrier between himself and the young. The young were impenetrable. They didn't think as he did. That is, assuming they thought at all. He was old and belonged to an old continent and an old religion. These usually solitary lunches of his had afflicted him with speculation—another of the disasters of old age. He put his long, thin nose down to his plate.

And sitting opposite him now was a man Bernard didn't know at all but was going to have to trust. At some point. Pray God not yet. And could he be trusted?

What was an American soul really like? Like a supermarket, where you could get anything from anywhere? Was it always sunlit and fresh? Could you find ghosts on its shelves? What else but ghosts were in the Belgian soul? Dead, wretched blacks in the Congo, Germans garroted, Jews sent to the SS barracks in Mechelen, Emma standing up with her hands clasped before her, saying by her every exhausted gesture, by her stance (both defiant and submissive): Do your worst, you can't touch me? Was the electric chair *serious*? Judicial murder any better than what Kekes had sought to do?

1.1. Magdalen

From the moment M. Forsell had walked into the Liegois, Bernard knew what he had come for. He wanted to do that wonderfully American thing—to lay his cards on the table.

He was astonished by the cards he held. A straight flush. The night up in the hills. An explanation for the inexplicable Andrzej. And when he had finished showing his hand all Bernard could reply—astonished and fascinated—was: *"C'est exact."* The basic facts were right.

Yes, he and Nous had agreed to fire in the air.

He couldn't say for sure that Nous had, but that was what he did.

Why?

Because we didn't agree with Tamas. Because we didn't like him. Because we saw what he really wanted—a mix of personal revenge and deadly political intent. Because it was too late to hunt down collaborators even if it was certain that they had collaborated. Because it was time to get back to our own lives. Because it is reprehensible to kill in cold blood, and even more reprehensible when the victim is young and a woman.

Bernard went on to say he didn't find the moral of defeat and occupation all that simple. Was I myself perfect? No, I did my share of favors and received favors in return. Everyone did. I'm no hero. And I found it revolting to see women—whores and housewives and mothers—shorn and marched through a jeering male population. Knowing what any one of them would have done for a chunk of sausage. The basic rule was survival. Everyone was hungry. So *Mevrouw* Kerkevelde sold shoes to the *Boches* and the big plants and mines here and elsewhere coughed up what the Germans would have taken anyway. Collaboration?

People who *betrayed*, that was another matter. And that's what Kekes did. He got rid of his ideological enemies in the party—or the people who stood between him and the power he so craved—and then got rid of those people who knew what he'd done.

How could I *not* participate?

To Bernard, this didn't need explaining. To start with, it had all happened very quickly. Kekes had called Nous. Gloating that now 'we' had her—That is, the British were sending her back. Nous called me. He said, What do we do? I said, Nothing. Then Emma escaped. I heard from Conincq that she was in bad shape and wanted to escape to Spain. Kekes got wind of that and said, If she tries to contact you, detain her.

She did contact you. So Conincq says.

I saw her, she went off. She went to the Pole and she must have been seen there. Kekes went down there with some of his 'lads' and there was an altercation. The Pole was hurt and Emma was bundled into a car. In a great hurry, we were summoned by telephone to a 'trial'. A trial by the Resistance. It was always a part of Kekes' plan that Nous and I should be made complicit. That we should share the guilt. That way, no awkward questions could be asked.

The trial had lasted twenty minutes. Kekes had ranted, his miners had the hall packed, the vote was unanimous: except for those who kept silent.

Pons said, Nous and I had about a minute outside to discuss our options while Kekes was getting Emma into the car. We could not shoot Emma, and kill Kekes instead. It would be an 'accident'. We agreed we would shoot in the air. About Kekes, we agreed we'd wait and see. I'm not proud about our hesitation. We weren't saving Emma's honor, but our own. How else could we stand up for Emma? Kekes had us over a barrel. By the end of the war, he was drunk with power and anticipation. The Russians were marching on Berlin, soon they'd be *here*! I was a man of the right, a man of the Church. If I refused to do my 'duty,' the reason would be that I too was a fascist. At the Liberation, you didn't need evidence. All you needed to do was point a finger. Taad was in the same position. Taad grew rich on the favors he did—I might add, with an even hand—for the local authorities and certain German officers.

Thank you, Henning said. That clarifies certain things. What happens to Kekes now?

Nothing. The *Commissaire* has pulled him in for questioning.

Kekes won't talk and there is no possibility whatsoever that they can hang the killing on him. There's not a single reliable witness and his people will swear on the heads of Marx and Lenin that he was somewhere else. No, I believe they call it a 'drive-by shooting' in your country, M. Forsell.

Henning said, One last question. You seem absolutely neutral about Emma. I mean, however desirable she might be, she was on the other side, wasn't she? Supported the fascists, paraded with them… There's even the suggestion she took part in an unsavory affair in Courcelles. You were in the *maquis*, you were fighting against her.

I fought against the Germans, not against fascism. Just as I'd fight against Bolsheviks, but not against the Russians. Our local Rexists—the people Emma took up with—were in some cases thoroughly appalling people, some Nazis, some sadists, but most weren't. Some were reformers. Many of them were patriots. The choices Belgians had to make, in such a small country, were inordinately difficult. France had collapsed, we didn't; but half of France was 'free', none of this country was. We 'French' Belgians, the Walloons, had nothing to fall back on; our Flemish brothers—if you can call them that—were made of the same stuff as Germans. It was common for the politically naive to believe a New Order was indeed coming in Europe.

Henning said ruefully, You could have said all of this some weeks ago when we first met. You weren't playing fair with me.

Why should I have helped you? I am accustomed to young gentlemen like yourself who are ever so eager to undo everything that my generation believed in. You will agree—no doubt in your country as in mine—that a mindless press belongs to the Left? Well, in their tiny brains, Hitler and the Jewish Question make everything that isn't on the Left suspect, while the crimes of the so-called Left—of the Bolsheviks and their friends abroad like Tamas Kekes—go not only unpunished, but unexamined. In the circumstances, would you have given aid and assistance to the enemy?

Bernard was grateful that—once again—he hadn't been forced to give away what really happened. He knew he would be, but so

Emma H.

far the defenses thrown up over the past thirty-eight years had held up pretty well. The real question was if the American knew he could be trusted.

If he couldn't be, Kekes would make sure that Emma died a second time.

Chapter twenty-two

It's not that difficult to get the Army List, Henning was to say. There's the British club system, the old boy network. Adam Lowry, the subaltern in a small town in Germany in 1945, went to a very minor public—that is, private—school. He's now a solicitor in Shropshire. And like everyone else who knew her, he remembered Emma.

What he said was simple. That he first thought maybe Emma was one of the camp survivors who had wandered off in a state of starvation, that she could have fallen in with other displaced persons. She certainly had no papers, and what's more, her memory seemed to have been affected. He saw plenty of that. Sometimes it was deliberate—a lot of people had things to hide—and sometimes it was part of the fortunes of war.

But the one thing Lowry remembers best is that despite her bedraggled clothes (ex-army trousers, a man's shirt) Emma 'sounded posh'. Educated. Upper class. Despite conditions in his holding camp, she remained very refined in her behavior and Lowry did not think she was faking amnesia.

In short, he was smart enough to pick her out and refer her

Emma H.

case—the record of her interrogations and a photograph—to British headquarters in Hanover. As Emma H., because she wasn't able to provide any information about her family or where she came from.

She did, however, speak fluent French, Flemish and German. Good enough English and some Russian.

She struck Lowry from the start as a 'difficult case,' but given the number of displaced persons passing the frontier in both directions and the volume of work involved in identifying war criminals and collaborators, he said he didn't expect an early answer.

He was therefore surprised when headquarters replied within a week and asked him to ascertain if Emma H. had been accompanied by anyone when she had been held up at the frontier. He was able to answer by telephone that she had been alone: 'alone, distracted and confused.'

Lowry thought nothing would come of the inquiry. Emma H. was very young for a suspect. Furthermore, she had come from the East—not from Belgium or France—and had made several references to having been (she thought) in Berlin.

The day he made that telephone call, Lowry had called her into his office and asked her if she'd come alone.

Yes, she said.

From Berlin? She thought so.

And what had she been doing in Berlin? Escaping.

Escaping from what?

From them.

Who were they? The Bolsheviks.

Lowry said, Then she asked me to refer her case to 'the General'.

'What general?'

The one who was in Berlin.

She said something about selling a last jewel and the wife of the general. She described a house where she'd seen the general.

Then I went to England, Henning said. England meant the awesomely grand 'cottage' near Maidenhead where Lady Bodkin—once a Polignac princess and now the ninety-something widow of

I.I. Magdalen

Sir Hugh Bodkin—had been living since her husband's recent death. The one who was in Berlin then, General Bodkin.

 The outside, seen through curtains of old lace and the French doors of her drawing-room, was green and wet. The lawns ran down to vague misty water below and I expected (Henning said) the General to come through those French windows and sit down by the fire with the hem of his baggy trousers wet and mud on his riding boots. Because no doubt he'd been out walking the dogs in what was far more than a foggy, foggy dew. Not so. The general was gone, the dogs were sprawled by the fire and Lady Bodkin was in a talkative mood.

 She'd known Emma's family from before the war ("bforthwah"). The Hoofrads are—*were*—related in one of those obscure ways families have. She remembered her perfectly. Both as a child (an extraordinarily self-contained child, very proper, very well turned-out) and as the woman who'd hidden with her companion in a room over what had once been the stables in 1945.

 She said, Hardly the sort of person one would turn away. Um. Once one knew who she was. That is, cook came in indignantly to tell me she'd found a young woman going through our rubbish bins. Early May it was. I said, Bring her in. My husband could be peremptory and I felt sorry for the civilians in Berlin—especially the women.

 So Emma came in. I wouldn't have recognized her. God only knows what she'd been through or who she was or why she was hiding in our stables or how she managed that. All I saw was a young woman—Well you know how dust and dirt and hard times can age a face, so she didn't look that young—wearing bits of uniform, field gray patches on her trousers, old jumper sleeves as stockings, shoes held with string. It was late spring, clothing was clothing. People in Berlin made out with what they could find.

 I said, Explain yourself. Or something like that.

 She said, We'll go. Just don't turn us over to the Military Police.

 Naturally, I wanted to know why she'd come to our house. If she and this man were running away from something—everyone was—the house of a British general wasn't what I would have chosen.

I told her I'd said nothing about handing her over to the police, I just wanted to know what she was doing in my house.

She was reluctant to say. Exhausted, I supposed. You met many people like that in Berlin. People with nothing left to say. What had happened was something they couldn't even explain to themselves.

I said, Take your time. No harm will come to you here.

I rang for the maid and asked her to tell cook to make some sandwiches and tea.

I asked, Who is the man cook says has been with you? Are you married?

No.

Are you German?

No.

I said, Bring him here. Your man.

He's gone. He left two days ago. He was only here one night.

You didn't come together.

No.

You only just met?

No. We agreed to meet. *If* we reached Berlin.

To meet in my house? I didn't want to press the poor creature and it was only then that I realized I'd been talking to her in English and she'd been replying in English. Was she English? If so, it made some sense to come to the British zone. I brought her over to the window so that I could have a better look at her. Then I saw that really she wasn't a woman at all. She was a body. Dressed in rags and with nothing human left about her. I saw right away then what had happened to her. She must have arrived in Berlin from somewhere or other—fleeing the Russians, caught up with the routed remains of the German army, squeezed somewhere—and like thousands of others would have been walking through the rubble with no idea where she was going.

I knew what had happened. To *any* woman. She'd been

raped, of course. A common enough story. One asked of one's friends—decent Germans one might have known long before—not what happened but how many times? Women of my age, of any age. Grandmothers and schoolchildren. The answers ran—when one could get an answer—from five to fifty. One wondered how those women could still talk. The Russians, you know.

But very calm, this one was. For someone in her position. Still, you could see it in her eyes. She was absent, passive, submissive, as though it had all happened to someone else. Remote from reality, that's how she impressed me. Holed up somewhere inside herself. Can't blame her. Found it hard to blame anyone and I can't tell you how happy we were to be moved from Berlin to Hanover. Still rubble. But not this kind of human rubble.

Tell you the truth, Henning said, I found it a suffocatingly civil and diffident way of talking. Little brittle and indifferent fragments of some horrible story that was bound to end up in death.

I said, I'm a plain man. Could you tell me what happened?

She stiffened a bit, as though I'd committed a *faux pas*, but then she said, well, at first I was thinking mainly how furious Hugh—my husband—would be that civilians had been hiding in our quarters. Hugh was a dear man and I miss him, but he was very military in his way of looking at things. One sometimes felt human beings didn't matter. He'd been in Ireland, you see, in the Troubles.

I said I was sorry. Not about Ireland. I hadn't meant to be abrupt. Emma had been going through the garbage?

Lady Bodkin said, For something to eat. It turned out the staff knew they were there, Emma and her man. Hans—our interpreter—had a room back there himself. He'd walked in on them, curled up on the floor like old carpets or blankets in an attic, which is what he thought they were. Until he noticed the blankets or carpets were breathing regularly.

That seemed to strike a chord with Lady Bodkin, as though it were some schoolgirl escapade. She said, They were just trying to keep *warm*. There was no heat in the stables. You have to remember they'd escaped just ahead of the Russians. On the run all the time. It was a bitter winter to be beaten in. After that, Hans brought them food he saved off his plate. It couldn't last. Hans had to go off with my husband for a few days. Hence the rooting about in the rubbish.

And then Emma said who she was?

Cook was very upset. She was afraid I would accuse her of stealing. No, she didn't say anything about who she was until the maid brought in tea and sandwiches. She sat down and ate them without appetite. Almost mechanically. Like the not-quite-dead. We were like two people who meet at some lugubrious function and don't know quite what to say to one another. Could I ask you to poke the fire?

I did, Henning said. The conversation went on at its choppy pace. Lady Bodkin was after all a grand old lady. Cook was called 'Cook'. Rape was rape even on the forty-ninth or fiftieth time. I thought of her German ladies. Respectable. Known no doubt—some of them—since boarding school. Which was where she met Isbel Kerkevelde.

Thank you, she said.

One felt sorry for her. I mean as a child. Her parents and that pretty Swedish queen dead. She'd spent a month with my grandchildren in Antibes. Very pretty child in an odd sort of way. Some might have said stuck up. Went to church every day, I remember. Our *Mademoiselle* was something of a free thinker and had to go with her. You see I'm not sure she knew who she was or where. I thought, if I ask for her story, I'll fall into it headfirst and never get out of it again. It will be another *imposition*. But then she brought it up herself.

Who she was?

Not so directly as that. I forget what we were talking about—I suppose, as usual, I was doing most of the talking—when she said something like, But surely Tante Constance. That brought us both up sharp.

I looked into those astonishing green eyes of hers and said, Do I know you?

You used to. After my parents died.

Of course, I said. Emma. Emma Hoofrad.

You see, she admitted that. But not as though it counted for anything. Not as though it gave her any special right. Just enough to throw us into French and for her to say, Don't worry, I don't want anything from you.

Tragic, really. But then she wouldn't be the first pure girl to go disastrously wrong, would she? But then not many do so willfully.

It wasn't true either. She did want something from me. She wanted me to help her sell a jewel. She said it was her last one. It didn't matter what happened to her but her man…He had to get to Spain. He'd already left, but they were supposed to meet up—She didn't say where. It was *his* decision. She would have a better chance if she were alone.

A better chance of what? I asked.

Of getting away.

Kloosters, I said.

Lady Bodkin waved the name away. She said, I never knew who he was. It was as though she were talking about a servant she'd dismissed.

Emma knew what their situation was. They weren't just a part of that ghostly army that had folded back into Germany. They were foreigners there, bearers of ill tidings, unauthorized victims, *volunteers* for this particular disaster.

You have to understand, the whole conversation was intensely strange. We sat there in her drawing room, no one turned the lights on. We talked by the light of the fire in a dank English autumn afternoon. Lady Bodkin was immaculate. Sort of corrugated, as you'd expect at her age, silver hair crimped, a smell of powder, bright lips. Conversation died down—like the fire—and then revived again, when poked.

Lady Bodkin said, Naturally, we couldn't take her jewel. It would have put us in a very false position. That is, I knew who the girl had been—a bereaved summer guest, girls playing together in Antibes, the daughter of a school-mate, old loyalties, and something very Catholic (though Isbel was one of a handful of Protestant girls at school)—but I had no idea who she was *now* or what she'd been in the decade between 1935 and 1945. None. I told her I would let her have some money, pounds, and a few frocks. You know, something to get on with. I told her people often had lives to re-make and she was still young—pathetically young, I thought, pathetically young to look so old.

Then Hugh came back. I was still talking to her when he walked into the room. She was up immediately like a jack-in-a-box. She mumbled some excuse and ran out the door past Hugh before I could even introduce her.

I don't suppose Hugh would have remembered her. But later in Hanover when the papers came through that she'd been stopped at the border Hugh said, A camp follower, foolish girl. Dressed like a man. What sort of girl would do that? Hugh called it 'coming to a sticky end'. That's what happened to Irish Republicans. Naturally, he had some high moral view about it. About how bad things lead to bad ends. Poor Hugh! His descriptions were always terse, and he never had any idea that women can understand things…I mean politics and things of that sort.

He said, We've looked into it. Into her case and his. What's his name? I don't doubt they fought for what they believed in. But one doesn't change sides.

I thought she was more unfortunate than anything else and said so.

I asked if she'd seen Emma again after that. After her husband came home.

No. I told you, I thought she was unfortunate. But also that she accepted her fate. She took responsibility for what she'd done, whatever that was. You know what I think, looking back on those matters now? I think it's possible she had a death wish. That she didn't want to live. That was the feeling I had when Hans and I went up to her room the next day. The dresses I'd sent up to her with my maid were—all but one—thrown down on the floor. Also the pounds in an envelope—they were laid out on her pillow. On the envelope she'd written neatly, I don't deserve your charity. Gone. Quite gone. It was a shock. It weighed on my mind. That she would still be wandering.

I said, You had no inkling about the man she was with? How they felt about each other?

I think they were comrades, she said. Comrades-in-arms. Terrible things had happened to them and around them. They got through them together.

A maid about as old as Lady Bodkin brought in drinks and turned on a single standing lamp in a faraway corner.

I said, Her papers eventually came before your husband? He would have talked to you about her. At the end, when she was caught at the border. I talked to the officer who was holding her.

Hugh didn't discuss business at home. Army business. It isn't done. Just general things. I *asked*. Hugh was reluctant to talk about it. We've been through this before, he said. Emma wasn't the only case, you know. People got caught up one way or another. People we'd known socially. Cousins even. There wasn't much Hugh could do. There was policy and there were people. So many people claimed to have lost their papers.

There was no direct appeal to your husband?

Lady Bodkin said, My impression was that she wasn't the sort who appealed.

No, probably not, I said.

Later, Hugh said he would have liked to do something for her, but there were rules and he couldn't change them. He said I would have to trust him. There had been a careful inquiry.

She escaped. She must not have trusted the inquiry.

If she had trusted it, her case would at least have been handled officially.

We were both tiring and some of the time it seemed Lady Bodkin was lost in her own thoughts.

I said, You never heard from Emma again? Nor from her aunt, Berthe? Or her notary, a M. Conincq? Her godfather? No one told you, no one appealed to you?

Yes. I seem to remember Hugh getting a letter in Hanover and telling me about it or perhaps about someone who had come to see

Emma H.

him. I don't think he was annoyed. He just didn't feel that it was right to mix personal feelings or loyalties with what was right and proper. Least of all towards someone who hadn't shown that sort of care with the feelings of others. He said the case against her was a serious one. Her man—the one who arrived in Berlin with her—had got to Spain along with the leader of the Rexists, Léon Degrelle. He—you may remember—had crashed his plane on the beach in San Sebastian. Nor had the two of them reached Berlin from Russia. They'd been in a chateau in Belgium throughout the last offensive in the Ardennes. Die-hards both of them.

Why was it I didn't entirely believe her? Or feel there was something she was holding back? The sphere she and her husband had lived in wasn't my sphere, and she and her husband had had long experience in dealing with importunate questions. I remember walking back to the car I'd hired, hearing the wet gravel crunch under my feet, and thinking that for her these were *family* matters. About which one did not speak to strangers. And if her husband had been stern and upright did that mean that she had been?

I couldn't put a finger on it then, but I had this sort of dim instinct that it had not been General Sir Hugh Bodkin who'd talked to Emma's emissary, but Lady Bodkin herself.

Maybe it was the way we parted at the door. The way she said, So nice to have met you. And so kind of you to take an interest in the poor child.

Chapter twenty-three

A strike of air-controllers—in France of course—had made it impossible to fly directly back to Belgium, and Henning overnighted in Frankfurt and took the train back to Liège, where he was to meet up with Ludi, via Köln. Travel—even disrupted, uncomfortable travel—had always been his down-time, his thinking time. He loved long waits in airport lounges and bars, the blank faces of travelers trapped in their sealed 3,000-foot-high cabins, the anodyne interruptions of pilots, the anonymity of the service in first class conducted by stewardesses well past their prime. He loved expressionless airport hotels, their tasteless dinners and slow German breakfasts reached in elevators smelling of morning farts. Likewise, the long, sparkling ride to the Frankfurt *Hauptbahnhof.* And nothing beat the steady diesel-hum of trains, the plush gray seats, the pile of newspapers by his side and the landscape—so organized—slipping past his window into oblivion.

Ah, 'Enning, Ludi said, waiting for him at the hotel. You have finished with this girl?

Emma H.

Finished? He thought of the list he'd written on the train. A list of liars.

Just about. Would you mind terribly if we dined with a *Commissaire* of the Belgian Police? He's a nice man, but he avoids the truth. I have an idea in the back of my head. I think I have been very stupid not to think of it before.

The dinner was excellent, the *Commissaire* in good form, Ludi chatty and Henning went straight (well, almost) to his point. First he gave Masquelier an abbreviated account of his interview with Lady Bodkin (*Ah, les anglais*, said the *Commissaire*) and then he said straight out that if everyone was lying about Emma—well not lying but omitting some essential fact—in his own way the *Commissaire* too had hardly been forthcoming with the truth.

The *Commissaire* didn't even blink.

He said, You are quite right. Pre-va-ri-ca-tion. I did—prevaricate. There are some things I thought it best not to go into too deeply. I had my reasons.

Well, OK. There are all sorts of things people don't really want to know about. Exactly when you're going to die, what your parents do in bed. So you've short-changed the truth. And now?

It felt bittersweet to Masquelier to be so near the end. To have yielded territory so grudgingly and find himself left with truth as his only option. Frankly, the dinner—and its underlying argument—reminded him of his youth. While enjoying looking at the lovely young wife, he could also sense a long array of facts and talk and surmises working their way through the young American's mind. He had been in the same position when he began his career. The revelation that even very proper and decent people also cheated and stole and lied and occasionally killed—some reluctantly, others less so—had been hard to live with. And in time, he'd had to learn that a form of lying—of prevarication and self-protection—was as natural and necessary to the average human being as food and drink and fornication. If he hadn't done much outright lying himself back then, before the war, it was because he had a deadly fear of retribution.

He said, Our mutual friend Bernard Pons said to me long ago that in no way does Catholic doctrine consider lying a sin. Only under oath. He said that was why people like me were necessary. Or at least a *flic* of some kind. These people you accuse of lying are people—*bon Dieu*—I've known all my life.

It's not lies. It's omissions. Two notaries *and* Emma's aunt led me to believe Emma's estate had never been settled. I was a fool to take their word for it. I should have checked.

What could a simple *Commissaire* answer? Of course M. Forsell should have checked. But would he have found out? Or would further lies have been added to those that misled him from the start?

Henning said, You knew, didn't you?

No he didn't 'know' in that sense. He said, I knew there were a lot of greedy people around. I knew—no, I surmised—her aunt couldn't bear not knowing. That was why she wrote that open letter and presumably why she lured you here.

Still, it *was* settled, Henning said. The money isn't where Conincq and Emma's aunt say it is. I haven't had time to check since I got back.

It would have upset her to have so much money floating about unused. She has had to be a determined woman.

I think she must have hated Emma.

That is probably true, though 'hated' is perhaps not the right word. 'Envied' would be better. Envied her beauty, her money, her *clarity*. *Mevrouw* Kerkevelde was always very determined not to relinquish anything to anyone. That was what she learned as a girl. That everyone else in the family frittered things away: by getting themselves killed like her brother or by becoming an 'artiste' like her younger sister. The German *Kommandatur* loved her for that sheer determination. A determination in which morals counted for nothing. She didn't care that the Nazis were supposed to be bad people. What she focused on were her surreptitious barges, her false bills of lading, all that Jewish furniture that found its way to the good burghers of Frankfurt and Berlin. I knew about all that. Everyone knew about it. You've spotted the thread that holds the rosary beads together?

Emma H.

Rosaries and sore knees on stone floors, sisters, and sexual repression. That had been part of Masquelier's youth, too.

Henning said, I know nothing beats smooth words for hiding the truth. Such a classy, civil woman as Lady Bodkin must have—I reckon—some very pressing reason to stop short of the whole truth. At her level, you don't often have to lie to get what you want. Well? What could that lie be?

That they are all Catholics. Very much Catholics. The people on *your* list, starting with Lady Bodkin, no? The good father, the now-dead Pole, Bernard and so on. I have the other side. Kekes, Nous, Tante Berthe, Coquin. And you and I both start with the same simple fact.

That's right. There is no body. There is no place she's buried. There is no death certificate.

I didn't have to think about that. I knew there wasn't. Nor did the other people on your list have to think about that. They knew it too. But the people on my list didn't. You've put all these two-plus-twos into a reasonable argument?

I think so, said Henning. I mean, this is not a court of law, I am not a policeman, no one is to be charged with anything, so no evidence is really needed. I suppose I hope that one of the people in the second group will wish to tell me the truth, and I don't think it will be you, my dear *Commissaire*.

Pas à table, anyway. Not over a good meal.

Please don't misunderstand me, Henning said. I know you would like to tell me the truth. But I respect the fact that you have an official position.

Which I will be leaving in a few months.

To go fishing.

Exactly.

So I will talk to Bernard. Over another good meal.

That would be what I would do.

Ludi could not help herself. She said, And that's all there is to it? After that, it will all be over?

Henning said, I'm fairly sure Bernard wants to tell me. Am I right, *Commissaire*? I mean, all he wants to know is whether I can keep a secret. That's really what everyone on my list has wanted all along. And they're right. You have to know who you can trust.

The way I see it is that when we're young, we don't see how others perceive us. We don't know exactly what kind of *effect* we can have. For instance, when we start asking questions. Even in ordinary talk. We live in a lovely sort of blind ignorance. We think we are omnipotent. There are no bounds to the authority with which we see the real world. Alas! Other people have other ideas. It's very hard—if we think we're good people, doing God's work, not that God has a whole lot to do with the Police—to imagine that someone out there fears us or hates us enough to try to kill us. Emma was that sort of young woman. When you started asking questions you became that sort of person. Then I suppose it hit you—because you've only seen Kekes Tamas from a distance. And Bernard will tell you that even if he were sitting as close to you as I am, Kekes couldn't really see you.

Chapter twenty-four

The sun had come out, low at this time of year, carrying with it a scent of decaying pine. So this is what it all came down to, Bernard thinks. His life examining, theirs exhumed. Decades of silence. Lives archived and then extracted from dead papers and documents come across almost accidentally. Walking from Nous Taad's lodge toward the quarry feels like an exhumation. Which would be followed by an autopsy.

There had been an autopsy once, and an exhumation. He'd found the site in *his* archives among the War Burial Commission's reports, because nearby ten Jews had been hastily thrown into the quarry when it was dry in the summer of 1943. The Commission's work of un-burying had been done by German prisoners in the first months after the war. A grim irony.

In the same archives, he also found numerous Germans hastily buried in forests and barnyards. A lot were shallow-buried along the canals, because canals had footpaths along them. That was only fair. You buried all the dead of a war.

This site had been marked with a crude cross, one length of

birch nailed to another. Masquelier—then fresh back from the *Congo Belge*—several weeks before Emma came back to Liège—had ordered the autopsy.

He remembered the cold in the morgue, the big loose sweater he wore with its sleeves keeping his hands warm, and how had held his breath.

But the body itself, corrupt, and transported in a tarpaulin to a marble slab, had no scent at all. Little flesh remained attached to the bone after weeks had gone by. Most of it was attached to the skull, together with brief tufts of fair hair, which the pathologist in a long apron nipped off the cranium with tweezers.

No? Bernard said, seeing him hesitate.

I don't think so. About forty. Look at the pelvis. She had at least one child.

Bernard felt sorry for the nameless woman. He wondered about the child.

Had he been relieved the body wasn't Emma's? Yes, he had feared that. Others had come back from the war, people who'd done far worse things than Emma, but his god-daughter hadn't. She remained silent: among the missing. In the light of that, what did it matter what he had felt?

But today he is more or less at what he thinks is the spot— though the weird horizontal sunlight filtered through the wood is as misleading as the darkness and Kekes' flashlight had been accurate. That flashlight—Kekes thought as he walked on the uneven mud—had been *very* theatrical. If there were no sun, Bernard would be able to see the flashlight wavering left and right. It's *that* vivid in his mind.

From behind him he hears Jaap Fresco—the Cerberus of this particular hell—rev up his motorbike and then stop.

It occurs to Bernard that with Taad dead there is no one left for Fresco the watchdog to watch. He's old and he's become useless. Just as back then he'd been surly and useful. He did the dirtiest work, so strong were his hatreds.

I.I. Magdalen

Bernard retraces his steps, scuffing wet leaves with his shoes. He says to Fresco, I told you to get out.

Fresco says, I'm going.

As he starts to step away, Bernard sees Fresco as a young man. Even then, he'd walked on his heels, tilted back, as if a part of him wanted to go in the opposite direction.

And Inspector Masquelier in those days had ears that stuck out like the vanes of a mill. Now they fitted sleekly close to his skull. Had that operation been based on sheer vanity, to get such prominences back to anonymity?

Bernard thinks, Masquelier never married either. Neither of us had much of a private life to be vain about.

He'd met with Masquelier as recently as yesterday.

He said, He (meaning Henning Forsell) has been poking around Nous' lodge with his wife. He would have no idea that was where Jaap *lived*. As you and I know, for services rendered to Nous. At various times. That's not safe. Get him out.

Yes, Bernard thinks. Yesterday's bee in the *Commissaire*'s bonnet was, Nothing says Kekes didn't get Jaap to kill Nous. That's right up Jaap's alley. We would need both our hands to count the times he did it back then. Germans sometimes.

Oh, not always, Bernard had replied.

Certainly not always Germans, the *Commissaire* had said.

Masquelier went on, as if the other kind weren't to be counted. They no longer mattered. He said—hands behind his back as they walked out of the Liegois—On the other hand we don't have a shred of evidence and Jaap's wife swears he was with her. She says his garage was open. And it was. I checked myself. Several people remember talking with him.

Now Bernard says to Fresco—This time in Flemish so Jaap won't tune him out, so he would really understand—He'll be here any minute now. He's meeting me here.

Jaap shifted backwards on his heels, a large man.

And stay away, Bernard says. Nous is dead. The Police don't

want you here. I don't want you here. We don't want you here. Those days are all over.

He hasn't heard that tone of command in his voice since the war. Nor has anything happened since the war. He blinks and thinks: just like that I'll be seventy. They'll want me to retire. Only rarely will anyone come up to consult the archive in my mind.

Jaap doesn't move. He's always been truculent. He says, Who are you to give orders round here? I thought you said the war was over.

Even in the chilly air, Jaap's pea jacket is unzipped. His belly hangs out.

Bernard says, *He's* a Red Indian. You know what that is? You won't even see the knife, he's that quick. Take my word for it. And when *ons kommissaris* lets him out, tell Kekes not to come back here either.

Then Bernard thinks he hears a car down below. He turns away from the sullen Fresco and starts walking again. He wants a last few minutes to think out what he is going to say and if what he is going to do is right or not. One last time.

Jaap throws the keys with fury. They land with a leafy jingle just behind Bernard. He shouts, I'll be back.

A moment later, Bernard hears the motorcycle bump and squeak down the narrow gravel road, the throttle roar on the main road.

Then everything grows very quiet. The forest becomes indoors: fresh needles underfoot like parquet, the sun going down as on a dimmer. He shivers.

Just about here, he thinks. This is more or less where Nous and I stood and argued. And I've not been here once since. Then he re-reads in his mind the letters Emma sent him in those last days. When she was so clear in her head as to her *desires*. God may not grant them, she said. But whatever happens, look after Andrzej. There's only so much a man like him can bear. She has only a pencil to write with! Not even a sharp one! She writes, Anyone would be glad to be granted such a clear choice and have no say in the choosing. I'll be alive or I'll be dead. That makes it easy.

Bernard thinks, capricious little girl, eager learner, superior heart, selfish, charitable—all those things. Saint, fox, close, far away. Some letters about nothing at all, 'Dear Godfather, Today I…'; others about her doubts and God, about music and the desire to be swept away; still others about obedience and authority and men who were strong and brave. What time in life is ever so rich and contradictory as adolescence? There, Bernard thinks, is the root of his sadness—that it should all come to so sudden an end, and with no explanations at all possible, to anyone, for anything.

Then Bernard is back arguing with Nous.

Nous says, let's kill the bastard.

Bernard hears himself say, No, not yet. Because he's heard a car (cars?) below. If need be, I can shoot him. Whose cars are they? More of Kekes' fanatics? The police? The Pole?

Kekes is less than ten yards ahead of them, and Emma some way ahead of him. Walking with her long strides. Accustomed to life and death.

Bernard thinks, Whatever she says about choices, if there's divine justice then it's better if the Pole and Father Krzysztof—He has sensed they can't be far away—can do what Emma *should* wish. Which is not to die a stupid, useless and undignified death. And Bernard doesn't doubt that God will have a hand in deciding.

He'd given his word to her back then, hadn't he! He'd said, No one will ever know. If God so allowed, she might be saved: in this world and the next.

Whereas Nous hadn't. Nous kept old stories locked up in a safe and gave his secretary the combination. Which was his bad luck.

This *feels* like the right place to meet the American. The forest is still. The quarry is deep. It is right to lay old specters to rest just where they had been so restless. In a way, he feels a certain pride. He is admitting the American into select company and he thinks Emma might not disapprove. It wasn't that Forsell had forced his way into that company. He and the *Commissaire* agreed the young man had a right of sorts to join them.

And poor Niemczyk. Bernard crosses himself.

The American found the manuscripts. Bernard never even thought to look for them.

There'd always been a conjecture that something had gone on between Andrzej and Emma that summer. But it was no more than a conjecture. No one had ever been able to ask the Pole about *anything*. He was too far gone. All Andrzej had ever been able to express—even at the end of his tether—was bafflement.

And Father Krzysztof, to round out the company. What Masquelier says is the American's list.

Well, the friar had exercised Christian charity.

He had talked to the little old bearded man in the convent parlor. A bag of bones by now. But firm. Even stubborn, the way Poles were. He said that only God kept secrets. Humans hid sins. That wasn't the same thing.

Now Forsell would be able to add himself to that list.

When he'd first turned up, the American said all he wanted to know was what kind of a woman Emma had been. That wasn't true. It wasn't knowledge he'd wanted and it wasn't just a want. It was a longing. Didn't that gave him certain rights?

That is what it all comes down to.

It is getting dark. A ring of sun through the trees becomes a spot, like when you turn off the television. Bernard strains his ears. Cars go by below. But not the way cars slow down and shift gears when they address the steep hill, the way the cars had on that night as Emma strode ahead of Kekes, and Kekes' flashlight wavered, and he and Nous argued.

It had been with relief that Bernard had heard the cars slow and shift down and make their way up the hill. He didn't want Kekes' blood on his hands. He didn't want any blood on his hands. There had been enough of that.

Young Inspector Masquelier to the rescue.

I.I. Magdalen

The three of them fired. Emma fell to the ground and Kekes stumbled away with his flashlight.

Looking up through branches, Bernard sees the last yellow light go and give way to the purple of dusk.

Forsell is there at last. His car is on its way up. Its wheels spin on loose gravel, then its lights overtake the dusk and light the lower branches of the trees.

Bernard turns back towards the lodge.

The engine is still running when he gets there and the American stands athwart its headlights with his hands in his jacket pockets. Seen in profile like that, Forsell's face reorganizes itself in Bernard's mind the closer he gets. What had seemed a blob of features, a general sandiness, switches to sharp edges: a nose like an adze, flint in the mouth, clear blue eyes, like an anatomist's scrutinizing an organ. Henning makes him think of a savage, painfully domesticated.

Both men hold out their hands at exactly the same moment.

Bernard speaks first. He says, I've brought you her answers. You agreed to the conditions.

I'll say nothing. Nobody will ever know.

No one ever said 'never', Bernard answers. One day you can tell the story. Though it will not be complete.

You think she deserves to be remembered?

I think she deserves to be remembered.

OK.

Shall we go inside? It's getting cold and Fresco left the heat on. I should turn it off when we leave. Masquelier will see our cars outside when he comes. That way he'll know we're both still here and things are all right.

They are, aren't they? says Henning. His voice holds no excitement. If anything, Bernard reflects, a tinge of sorrow. Perhaps because he wouldn't see her. Ever.

In ordinary life, they're fine. Isn't that what counts?

They sit in the kitchen, where a kerosene fire flickers and makes puckering noises.

Henning says, I could use a drink.

Bernard rummages about in the cupboards and finds a near-empty bottle of Poire from which he pours two glasses. He says, You asked if she was there against her will. She says, 'No.'

Henning nods.

I supposed that, Henning says. I never doubted that.

Never wondered?

Not once I started thinking she must be alive.

You asked if she went there of her own free will. Again, she says 'No.' The three of them took her there—the Pole, Father Krzysztof, our friend the *Commissaire*. She made her real decision after.

Could she have left?

Of course. Time passes, people forget. It takes five years to take final vows. Then your body, your soul and your fortune *belong*. Any time before that, all she had to do was let anyone of us know. Conincq would have found a way.

My third question?

If in retrospect she would change any part of her life? Another 'No'.

You believe her?

Deeply. Otherwise I wouldn't be here.

Nothing? *Nothing* she would change?

Henning takes a deep breath and then falls still before saying, So she's still alive.

Oh, I didn't see her, you know. That's not allowed. It took some time—and Father Krzysztof's intervention—before she admitted she might owe us even that much explanation. She answered, or so the good friar says, out of humility.

Not long after, the *Commissaire* arrives. He bows to the two men. It is not something he usually does. His bow reminds Henning of a derrick.

Henning says, I will inform her aunt that her niece is dead. That is, gone from this world. I won't be lying. As to the money…

The *Commissaire*—having found himself a third glass and

still bowing—says, In America you say something about two birds and one stone? In French we start with the stone: *'Faire d'une pierre deux coups.'* We use one stone to strike twice. I think you made an excellent stone.

Henning says, I think M. Conincq knows how to look after himself and will be able to explain to Tante Berthe. I called him up before leaving. He'll tell her it was one of Emma's many magnificent gifts, that she also paid to restore the organ he plays.

Masquelier adds—it is a mere aside—You know, he is old and quite possibly wise.

And the morals? Henning asks, turning to Pons.

Bernard thinks a moment. What does morality have to do with exceptional beings and exceptional lives? In his eyes, Emma's was one of these and not just for her physical beauty. She'd lived her life *absolutely* and to its logical end. Compared to that, the word 'morals' only expresses commonly held views, a sort of social lowest common denominator. When he was young himself, Bernard had thought he might lead such a life, and such a life would lead him to God, who made *absolute* demands. What belongs to another world is necessarily opaque, and—as Emma seemed to have understood from the start—sins and suffering and all, only God understood.

He says, Emma was always attracted to uncommon views. Even now. She believes in God. And she was attracted to failure. We were a sorry lot with our silly 'principles' about daily life and politics and war. She was in a world above that. Certain things were evil, if they were godless. God's causes are all lost causes. Think of her men. She wasn't attracted at all to Nous. She felt deeply for the Pole and she marched off to Russia on a truly lost cause. Perhaps with Andrzej and Poland in her mind. With someone, Kloosters, who believed in the same lost cause. Is that moral?

Henning, too, thinks about that. The morals? What morals? Emma had a life. That's what morals are.

He says, It seems I am going to be a father.

Emma H.

Masquelier raises his glass and says, May he grow up like his father.

I would hope not like mine. And your father? he asks Masquelier.

Mine fished also. But in different waters.

Bernard says, Mine never asked questions.

To which Henning answers, And mine left them all unanswered.

They all agree, moving towards their separate cars, it is probably better that way.

About the Author

Keith Botsford

I.I. Magdalen (pronounced Maudlin) is the alter ego used by Keith Botsford for what he, like Graham Greene, thinks of as 'entertainments'—stories of espionage and crime. Having been trained at law and once served in Counter-Intelligence, he has long specialized in crime stories in stints at *The Sunday Times*, *The Independent* and *la Stampa*. He finds the strong narrative sense of crime stories refreshing. When he is not writing, he is a professor of journalism and history in Boston; and when not in Boston, is in Uzes, France. *Emma H.* is the second of six stories featuring Henning Forsell, whose "business" is the history of crime, and whose passion is the motivation of ordinary people pushed to extremes.

The fonts used in this book are from the Garamond family

Other works by I.I. Magdalen published by *The* Toby Press

Lennie & Vance & Benji

as Keith Botsford (fiction)

The Mothers
Out of Nowhere
Editors by Saul Bellow and Keith Botsford (anthology)
Sixth Form 1939 by Marcella Olschki,
translated by Keith Botsford

The Toby Press publishes fine writing,
available at bookstores everywhere. For more information,
please contact *The* Toby Press at www.tobypress.com